The Dante Inferno:

Rafe's Temporary Fiancée

The Dante Dynasty Series:
Book #6

by

Day Leclaire

USA Today Bestselling Author

For more information, please visit my website:

http://www.DayLeclaire.com

Book Description

His fake fiancée... It's time for lone wolf Rafe Dante to feel the fiery power of The Inferno. After a disastrous first marriage to his non-Inferno wife, he's done with happily-ever-after. To satisfy his matrimonial-minded family, he hires a woman to fake an engagement, claiming they've experienced the burning itch of The Inferno. His plan is to pay his fiancée to leave him at the altar, and since Dante legend alleges The Inferno only ever strikes once, he'll finally be free to return to his lone wolf ways, problem solved. Only one slight glitch...

The minute he and his temporary fiancée touch, The Inferno strikes—for real.

Sweet, innocent Larkin Thatcher longs for a family of her own. Unfortunately, it isn't likely to happen, not considering the secrets she hides. When Rafe hires her to be his pretend fiancée and offers a place to stay, it's a godsend for both Larkin and her "dog," a lovely Husky who looks suspiciously like a wolf. But falling in love with his family while lying to them isn't part of the plan. Nor is the overwhelming desire that sparks between the two, one that threatens their plan to go their separate ways.

If she must leave, she will, even if it means she'll be homeless again, but not without an antique bracelet in Rafe's possession that will identify her father. It's all she wants from her soon-to-be-ex fiancé. All Rafe wants from her is, well ... *her*. At least, for now. But The Inferno has a funny way of turning "now" into forever.

What will happen when Rafe learns her true identity? Will "now" turn to never? Or will The Inferno find a way to mate these two lone wolves?

Dedication

To my wonderful readers who have been so encouraging through the years. My heartfelt thanks!

Table of Contents

Other Titles by Day Leclaire

The Dante Inferno:
The Dante Dynasty Series

Some blazes, once ignited, can't be extinguished. Just one burning touch connects a Dante with his soul mate. The Inferno ... curse or blessing?

Sev's Blackmailed Bride, Book #1

Marco's Stolen Wife, Book #2

Nicolò's Wedding Deception, Book #3

Lazz's Contract Marriage, Book #4

Luc's Unwilling Wife, Book #5

Rafe's Temporary Fiancée, Book #6

Draco's Marriage Pact, Book #7

Gianna's Honor-Bound Husband, Book #8

Becoming Dante: Gabe, Book #9

Dante's Dilemma: Romero, Book #10

Forever Dante: Lucia, Book #11

Chapter One

This time his family had gone too far.

Rafe Dante stared at the bevy of women being subtly—and not so subtly—paraded beneath his nose by various family members. He'd lost count of the number of women he'd been forced to shake hands with. He knew why they were doing it. They were all determined to find him a wife. He grimaced. No, more than just a wife.

They hoped to find his Inferno soul mate, a Dante legend that had gotten seriously out of hand. For some reason, his family had it fixed in their heads that it only took one touch for some strange mythical connection to be forged between a Dante and his soul mate. Ridiculous, of course. Didn't they get it?

Not only didn't he believe in The Inferno, but he had no interest in ever experiencing matrimonial blisslessness again. His late wife, Leigh, had taught him that lesson in the short span of time from "I do" to "My lawyer will be in touch." Of course, that phone call had never come. Eighteen months ago his wife had chartered a private plane to Mexico to recover from the tragedy of her marriage to him and met a far worse fate when her plane crashed into a mountainside, leaving no survivors.

Rafe's younger brother, Draco, joined him and folded his arms across his chest. He stood silently for a moment, surveying the room and the glittering contents, both jeweled and female. "Ready to surrender and just pick one?"

"Get serious."

"I am. Dead serious."

Rafe turned on his brother, only too happy to vent some of his irritation. "Do you have any idea what the past three months have been like?"

"I do. I've been watching from the sidelines, in case you hadn't noticed. I'm also keenly aware that once you succumb to The Inferno, I'm next in line for the firing squad. As far as I'm concerned, feel free to hold out as long as possible."

"I'm working on it."

Rafe returned his attention to the shimmer and sparkle and sighed. Dantes international jewelry reception possessed everything a man could ask for—wine, women and bling—and nothing he wanted.

The wine came from a Sonoma, California vineyard just a few hours from the family's San Francisco home office. He knew the label on the bottles was as exclusive as the guest list. The women were beautiful, wealthy, and shone as brilliantly as the wedding rings on display around the private showroom. As for the bling? Well, that often fell within his purview, at least it did when Dantes Courier Service transported the stunning array of gemstones and finished pieces.

And yet a sense of utter boredom nagged Rafe. How many times had he attended receptions similar to this one? Always observing. Always maintaining a vigilant eye from the shadows. Always the watchful lone wolf instinctively avoided by the guests, until one family member or another thrust a potential bride in his direction. It was a pattern that had repeated itself so many times he'd lost count.

This occasion celebrated the exclusive release of the latest Dantes collection, the Eternity line of one-of-a-kind wedding rings. Each unique set combined the fire diamonds for which his family was renowned with the Platinum Ice gold from Billings, the company owned by Rafe's sister-in-law, Téa Dante, who'd married his older brother, Luc, three months earlier. Just seeing rings that symbolized love and commitment filled Rafe with bitterness.

Been there. Done that. Still had the scars to prove it.

And then he saw her.

The little blonde pixie working the reception as one of the caterers couldn't claim the title of most gorgeous woman in the room, but for some reason Rafe couldn't take his eyes off her.

He couldn't say why she attracted his attention or explain the vague sizzle she stirred. Granted, her features were quite lovely, delicate and fine boned with enough whimsy to make them interesting. Maybe it was her hair and eyes—hair the same shade as the ice-white sand of a Caribbean island and eyes the glorious turquoise of the rolling ocean waves that splashed and frolicked across those pristine beaches. Then there was the sizzle he couldn't explain, a vague compelling itch urging him to get closer to her in every possible way.

She circulated through the display room of the Dantes corporate office building with a hip-swinging glide that made her appear as though she were dancing. In fact, she possessed a dancer's body, lean and graceful, if a bit pint-size, every delectable inch showcased by the fitted black slacks and tight red vest of her uniform.

She disappeared into the crowd, her tray of canapés held high, and he lost sight of her. For a split second he was tempted to give chase.

A few minutes later, the pixie waitress reappeared with a fresh tray of champagne and circled through the guests in the exact opposite direction from where he stood.

For some reason it annoyed Rafe. Determined to force a meeting, he began to maneuver his way through the crowd on an intercept course, one circumvented by Draco's restraining hand.

"What?" Rafe asked, lifting an eyebrow. "I'm thirsty."

Draco shot him a knowing look. "Funny. I'd have said you look hungry. And with so many eyes on you, I recommend you avoid sating your appetite until a more appropriate time and place."

"Hell."

"Relax. Where there's a will . . ." Draco gestured toward one of the nearby display cases and deliberately changed the subject. "Looks like Francesca's latest line of Eternity wedding rings is going to be a huge success. Sev must be thrilled."

Caving to the inevitable, Rafe nodded. "I think he's more thrilled about the birth of their son," he replied. "But this would probably rate as icing on the cake."

Draco inclined his head, then slanted Rafe a look of open amusement. "So, tell me. How many of the lovelies fluttering around the room have our beloved grandparents introduced to you so far this evening?"

Rafe's expression settled into grim lines. "A full dozen. Made me touch every last one of them, like they expected to see me set off a shower of fireworks or light the place up in a blaze of electricity or something."

"It's your own fault. If you hadn't told Luc you and Leigh never experienced The Inferno, the entire family wouldn't be intent on throwing women your way."

The fact so many of his relatives had succumbed to the family legend only added to Rafe's bitterness toward his own brief foray into the turbulent matrimonial waters. Time would tell whether their romances lasted longer than his own. They might claim they'd found their soul mates, courtesy of the Dantes' Inferno. Rafe, the most logical and practical of all his kith and kin, adopted a far simpler and pragmatic— okay, *cynical*—viewpoint.

The Inferno didn't exist.

No eternal bond established itself when a Dante first touched his soul mate, no matter what anyone claimed, any more than Dantes Eternity wedding rings could promise the marriages for which they were purchased would last for all eternity. Some hit it lucky, like his grandparents, Primo and Nonna. And some didn't, like the disastrous marriage to his late wife, Leigh.

Rafe stared broodingly at his older brother, Luc, and his bride of three months, Téa. They were dancing together, swirling across the floor, gazing into each other's eyes as though no one else in the room existed. Every emotion blazed in their expressions, there for the world to witness. Hell, even when Rafe had been in the most passionate throes of lust, neither he nor Leigh had ever looked at each other like that.

In fact, he'd been accused by the various women in his life that his penchant for practicality and hard, cold logic—his lone wolf persona—bled over into his personal life with dismaying frequency. Possessing a fiery passion in the bedroom definitely compensated, as did his striking Dante looks, they conceded, but not when that passion went no farther than the bedroom door. Emotionally distant. Unavailable. Intimidating. For reasons that bewildered him, the word always came accompanied by a shudder.

Why couldn't any of them understand he didn't do love? Not the brutal, I-married-you-because-you're-a-rich-and-powerful-Dante love his late wife, Leigh, had specialized in. Not the casual, melt-the-sheets-and-enjoy-it-while-the-bling-lasts type that characterized the women interested in an affair with him. And definitely not The Inferno brain-frying-palm-burning-happily-ever-after brand of bull spouted by his more emotional and passionate Dante relatives.

Rafe knew himself all too well. And he could state with absolute certainty he wasn't hardwired that way. He never had and never would experience an Inferno love.

Which was just fine by him.

"It was annoying the first few times they dangled a potential bride in front of me," Rafe informed his brother. "Since it Nonna and Primo did the dangling, I couldn't say much. But now everyone's gotten into the act. I can't move without having some gorgeous thing shoved under my nose."

Draco signaled to someone over Rafe's shoulder. "A fate worse than death," he said with a fake shudder.

"It would be if it were you under the gun."

"But I'm not." Draco leaned past Rafe and helped himself to a flute of champagne. "Want one?"

"Sure."

"Consider this your lucky day. The tray's right behind you." He offered a cocky grin. "And don't say I never did you a favor."

Confused by the comment, Rafe turned to take a glass and found his elusive pixie standing there, holding the tray of drinks. Up close he found her even more appealing than from across the room.

He gestured to her with the flute. "Thanks."

Her smile grew, lighting up her face, the room, and some cold, dark place in his heart. "You're welcome." Even her voice appealed, rich and husky with an almost musical lyricism.

Draco watched the byplay in amusement. "You know, if you want the relatives to leave you alone, there is one possible way."

That snagged Rafe's attention. "How?" he demanded.

Draco grinned. "Find your Inferno bride."

"Son of a—" Rafe bit off the curse. "I already told you. I'm never going to marry again. Not after Leigh."

He heard the pixie's sharp inhalation at the same time the flutes on her tray began to wobble unsteadily. The glasses knocked against each other, the crystal singing in distress. She fought to steady the tray, almost managed it, before the flutes tipped and cascaded to the floor. Glass shattered and champagne splattered in a wide arc.

Reacting instinctively, Rafe encircled the waitress's narrow waist and yanked her clear of the debris field. A tantalizing heat burned through the material of her uniform, rousing images of pale naked curves gilded in moonlight. Velvety-smooth arms and legs entwined around him. Soft moans like a musical symphony filling the air and driving their lovemaking.

Rafe shook his head, struggling for focus. "Are you all right?" he managed to ask.

She stared at the mess on the floor and nodded. "I think so."

She lifted her gaze to his, her eyes wide and impossibly blue, the only color in her sheet-white face. He didn't see any of the desire that had swept over him. Remorse and, oddly, a hint of panic, sure. But not so much as a flicker of passion. A shame.

"I'm so sorry," she said. "I started to step back so I could circulate some more and my foot slipped."

"You're not cut?"

"No." She blew out her breath in a sigh. "I really do apologize. I'll get this cleaned up right away."

Before she could follow through, another of the catering staff crossed the room to join them. He was clearly management, judging by the swift and discreet manner in which he took control of the situation and arranged to have the broken glass and champagne cleared away. The waitress pitched in without a word, but once she'd finished, the manager guided her over to Rafe.

"Larkin, you have something to say to Mr. Dante?" he prompted.

"I want to apologize again for any inconvenience I may have caused," she said.

Rafe smiled at her, then at the manager. "Accidents happen. And in this case, I'm the one at fault. I'm afraid I bumped into Larkin, causing her to drop the tray."

The manager blinked at that and Rafe didn't have a doubt in the world he'd have accepted the excuse if Larkin hadn't instantly protested, "Oh, no. The fault is entirely mine. Mr. Dante had nothing to do with it."

The manager sighed. "I see. Well, thank you for your gallantry, Mr. Dante. Larkin, please return to the kitchen."

"Yes, sir, Mr. Barney."

Rafe watched her walk away, still the most graceful woman in the room, at least in his opinion. "You're going to fire her, aren't you?"

"I wish I didn't have to. But my supervisor has a 'no excuses' policy for certain of his more exclusive clientele."

"I gather Dantes is on that list?"

Barney cleared his throat. "I believe you top the list, sir."

"Got it."

"It's a shame, really. She's the nicest of our waitresses. If it were up to me . . ."

Rafe lifted an eyebrow. "I don't suppose we can forget this incident took place?"

"I'd love to," Barney replied. "But there were too many witnesses and not all of our help is as kindhearted as Larkin. Word will get out if I turn a blind eye and then both of us will be out of a job."

"Understood. I guess it would have helped if she'd allowed me to take the blame."

"You have no idea" came the heartfelt response. "But Larkin's just not made that way."

"A rare quality."

"Yes, it is." Barney lifted an eyebrow. "If there's anything else you or anyone in your family needs . . . ?"

"I'll let you know."

The two men shook hands and Barney disappeared in the direction of the kitchen, no doubt to fire Larkin. Rafe frowned. Maybe he should intercede. Or better yet, maybe he could arrange for a new job. Dantes was a big firm with plenty of branches. Surely he could find an opening for her somewhere. Hell, he was president of Dantes Courier Service. He could invent a job if one didn't already exist. The thought of Larkin's sunny smile welcoming him to work each day struck him as appealing in the extreme.

Draco approached. "So? Have you given my idea any thought?"

Rafe stared blankly. "What idea?"

"Weren't you listening to me?"

"It usually works best if I don't. Most of the time your suggestions only lead one place."

Draco grinned. "Trouble?"

"Oh, yeah."

"Well, this one won't. All you have to do is find your Inferno bride and everyone will leave you alone."

Rafe shook his head. "Apparently, you're not great at listening, either. After that disaster of a marriage to Leigh, I'm never going to marry again."

"Who said anything about marriage?"

Rafe narrowed his eyes. "Explain."

"You know, for such a smart, analytical-type guy, there are times when you can be amazingly obtuse." Draco spoke slowly and distinctly. "Find a woman. Claim it's The Inferno. Maintain the illusion for a few months. Act the part of two people crazy in love."

Rafe's mouth twisted. "I don't do crazy in love."

"If you want everyone to leave you alone, you will. After a short engagement, have her dump you. Make it worth her while to go a long way away and stay there."

"You've come up with some boneheaded ideas in your time. But this one has to be the most ludicrous—" Rafe broke off and turned to stare in the direction of the kitchen. "Huh."

Draco chuckled. "You were saying?"

"I think I have an idea."

"You're welcome."

Rafe shot his brother a warning look. "If you say one word about this to anyone—"

"Are you kidding? Nonna and Primo would kill me, not to mention our parents."

"You?"

Draco stabbed his finger against Rafe's chest. "They wouldn't believe for one minute you were clever enough to come up with a plan like this."

"I'm not sure clever is the right word. Conniving, maybe?"

"Diabolically brilliant."

"Right. Keep telling yourself that. Maybe one of us will believe you. In the meantime, I have an Inferno bride to win."

Rafe headed for the kitchen. He arrived just in time to see Larkin refusing the wad of money Barney was attempting to press into her hand. "I'll be fine, Mr. Barney."

"You know you need it for rent." He stuffed the cash into the pocket of her vest and gave her a hug. "We're going to miss you, kiddo."

One by one the waitstaff followed suit. Then Larkin turned toward the exit and Rafe caught the glitter of tears swimming in her eyes. For some reason a fierce protectiveness swept through him.

"Larkin," he said. "If I could speak to you for a minute."

Her head jerked around, surprise registering in her gaze. "Certainly, Mr. Dante."

Instead of exiting into the reception area, he escorted her through the door leading to the hallway. "Is there a problem?" she asked. "I hope you don't blame Mr. Barney for my mistake. He did fire me, if that helps."

Ouch. "It's nothing like that," he reassured. "I wanted to speak to you in private."

Leading the way to the wing of private offices, he reached a set of double doors with a discreet gold plaque that read "Rafaelo Dante, President, Dantes Courier Service." He keyed the remote control fob in his pocket and the doors snicked open. Gesturing her into the darkened interior, he touched a button on a panel near the door. Soft lights brightened the sitting area section of his office, leaving the business side with its desk, credenza, and chairs in darkness.

"Have a seat. Would you like anything to drink?"

She hesitated, then gave a soft laugh. "I know I'm supposed to say no, thank you. But I'd love some water."

"Coming right up."

He opened a cabinet door concealing a small refrigerator and removed two bottles of water. After collecting a pair of glasses and dropping some ice cubes into each, he joined her on the couch. Sitting so close to her might have been a mistake. He could sense her in ways he'd rather not. The light, citrusy scent of her somehow managed to curl around and through him, along with the warmth and energy of her body. Light caught in her hair and left her eyes in dusky blue shadow. He'd hoped the business setting would dampen his reaction to her. Instead, the solitude served only to increase his awareness.

He gathered his control around him like a cloak, forcing himself to deal with the business at hand. "I'm sorry about your job," he said, passing her the water. "Firing you seems a bit severe for a simple accident."

"I don't normally work the more exclusive accounts. This was my first time." She made a face. "And my last."

"The catering firm won't switch you over to work some of their smaller parties?"

She released a sigh. "To be honest, I doubt it. The woman in charge of those accounts isn't a fan of mine right now."

"Personality conflict?"

The question made her uncomfortable. "Not exactly."

If he was going to hire her, he needed to gather as much information about her as possible, especially if she didn't deal well with authority. "Then what, exactly?" he pressed.

"Her boyfriend was on the waitstaff, and . . ." She trailed off.

"And?"

"He hit on me," Larkin reluctantly confessed.

"Something you encouraged?"

To his surprise, she didn't take offense at the question. In fact, she laughed. "JD doesn't require encouragement. He hits on anyone remotely female. I hope Janice figures out what a sleaze he is sooner, rather than later. She could do a lot better."

Rafe sat there for a moment, nonplussed. "You're worried about your supervisor, not your job?"

"I can always get another job, even if it's washing dishes," Larkin explained matter-of-factly. "But Janice's nice, when she's not furious because JD's flirting with the help. I just got caught in the middle."

Huh. Interesting assessment. "And now?"

For the first time a hint of worry nibbled at the corners of her eyes and edged across her expression. "I'm sure it will all work out."

"I overheard Barney say something about rent."

She released a soft sigh, the sound filled with a wealth of weariness. "I'm a little behind. What he gave me for tonight's work should cover it."

"But you need another job."

She tilted her head to one side. "I don't suppose you're hiring?"

He liked her directness. No coyness. No wide-eyed, gushing pretense or any sort of sexual over- or undertones. Just a simple, frank question. "I may have a job for you," he admitted cautiously. "But I'd need to run a quick background check. Do you have any objections?"

And then he saw it. Just a flash of hesitation before she shook her head. "I don't have any objections."

"Fine." Only, it wasn't fine. Not if she were hiding something. He couldn't handle another deceptive woman who faked innocence and then demonstrated avarice. Refused to deal with that sort of woman. "Full name?"

"Larkin Anne Thatcher."

She supplied her social security number and date of birth without being asked. He pulled out his cell and texted Dantes' head of security, Juice, with the request. He'd have gone through Luc, but there might be uncomfortable questions when he later presented Larkin as his Inferno bride. Better to keep it on the down low. In the meantime, he'd get some of the preliminary questions out of the way.

"Have you ever been arrested?" Rafe asked.

Larkin shook her head. "No, never."

"Drugs?"

A flash of indignation came and went in her open gaze before she answered in a calm, even voice. "Never. I've needed to take drug tests for various jobs in the past, including this latest one. I have no objection to taking one here and now if you want."

"Credit or bankruptcy issues?"

Indignation turned to humor. "Aside from living on a shoestring? No."

"Health issues?"

"Not a one."

"Military history?"

"I haven't served."

"Job history?"

Now she grinned. "How much time do you have?"

Rafe eyed her curiously. "That many?"

"Oh, yeah. The list is as long as it is diverse."

"Any special reason?"

She hesitated again, but he didn't pick up any hint of evasion, just thoughtfulness. "I've been searching."

"Right job, right place?"

She seemed pleased that he'd understood so quickly. "Exactly."

"I can't promise to offer that, but I might have something temporary."

For some reason she appeared relieved. "Temporary will work. In fact, I prefer it."

"Not planning on staying in San Francisco for long?" He tried to keep the question casual, but conceded that as attractive as he found her, he'd feel better about his proposition if she intended to move on a few months from now.

"I don't know. Actually, I'm looking for someone. I think he may be here."

"He." That didn't bode well for his little project. "Former lover?"

"No. Nothing like that."

He pressed. "Who are you trying to find?"

"That's not really any of your business, Mr. Dante," she said gently. "What I will tell you is that it won't have an impact on any job you might offer me."

He let it go. For now. "Fair enough."

His cell vibrated and he checked it, surprised to find that Juice had completed his preliminary check. Had to be a new record. Either that or Larkin Thatcher didn't have much history to find. The text simply said "Clean," but he'd attached an email that went into more specifics.

Rafe excused himself long enough to access his computer and scan it. Nothing unusual other than a long and varied work history. Considering she was only twenty-five, he found it rather impressive.

"Still interested in offering me a job?" she asked.

For the first time she betrayed a hint nerves, and it didn't take much thought to understand the cause. "How far behind are you on your rent?"

She tapped her pocket. "As I said, this will catch me up."

"But it won't leave you anything to spare for utilities or food, will it?"

She lifted a narrow shoulder in a wordless shrug that spoke volumes.

He took a moment to consider his options. Not that he had many. Either he made the offer and put Draco's plan into action, or he forgot the entire idea. He could still find a position for Larkin. In fact, didn't question he could do precisely that. The question was, which job?

If it weren't for the Parade of Brides, it would have been an easy question to answer. But the unpleasant truth was, he just didn't know how much more of his family's interference he could handle. It had gotten to the point where it didn't just interfere with his private life, but with his business one, as well. These days, he couldn't turn around without running into his many relatives. And for some reason, they were always accompanied by a young, single woman.

He needed it to stop. And soon.

Before he could decide, Larkin stood. "Mr. Dante, you seem hesitant." She offered an easy smile. "Why don't I make it easy for you? I really appreciate your concern, but this isn't the first time money's been tight. I'm sort of like a cat. One way or another, I always land on my feet."

"Sit down, Larkin." He softened the demand with a smile. "My hesitation isn't whether or not I have a job available for you. It's which job to offer."

She blinked at that. "Oh. Well, I can handle most general office positions, if that helps. Receptionist. File clerk. Secretary or assistant."

"What about the position of my fiancée?" He folded his arms across his chest and lifted an eyebrow. "Do you think you could handle that?"

Chapter Two

For a split second, Larkin couldn't breathe. It was as though every thought and emotion winked off.

"Excuse me?" she finally said.

"Yeah, I know." He thrust his hand through his hair, turning order into disorder. For some reason, it only added to his overall appeal. Before, he'd seemed a bit too perfect and remote. Now he looked wholly masculine, strong and authoritative with a disturbing edginess that most women found irresistible. "It sounds crazy. But actually it's fairly simple and straightforward."

Larkin didn't bother to argue. Nothing about this man struck her as the least simple or straightforward. Not the fact he was a rich and powerful man. Not his connection to one of San Francisco's leading families, the Dantes. Not his stunning good looks or the intense passion he kept so carefully hidden from those around him. How did the scandal sheets refer to him? Oh, right. The lone wolf who was also, ironically, the "prettiest" of the male Dantes.

True on both counts.

To her eternal regret, it was also true that he still loved his late wife so passionately, he never wanted to marry again. Too bad he'd married a woman who, while as beautiful to look at as the man pacing in front of her, possessed a single imperative—to take and use whatever she wanted in life, regardless of the cost or harm it might do others.

"I overheard you, you know," she warned. "I heard you tell your brother you never wanted to marry again. Not after Leigh."

"Leigh was my late wife," he explained. "And you're right. I don't ever want to marry again. But I do need a fiancée. A temporary fiancée."

She wasn't usually so slow on the uptake. Even so, none of this made the least bit of sense to her. "Temporary," she repeated.

He took the chair across from her and leaned forward, resting his forearms on his knees. Having him so close only made it more difficult to think straight. She didn't understand it. Of all the men in San Francisco, he should have been the very last she'd find attractive. And yet, every one of her senses had gone screaming onto high alert the instant he'd turned those brilliant jade-green eyes in her direction.

"You'd have to understand my family to fully appreciate my situation," he said.

Larkin fought to keep her mouth shut. How many times had she gotten herself into an awkward predicament because of her particular brand of frankness? More times than she could count. Despite her determination, a few stray words slipped out. "Your family does have a knack for hitting the gossip magazines."

To her surprise, he looked relieved. "Then you've read about The Inferno?"

"Yes." Excellent. She'd kept that both short and sweet, and yet truthful. Added bonus, he seemed pleased with her answer.

"Then I don't have to explain what it is or that my family—most of them, anyway—believe implicitly in its existence."

Something in his manner and delivery clued her in to his opinion of the matter. "But you don't?"

A wickedly attractive smile touched his mouth. "Have I shocked you?"

"A little," Larkin admitted. She couldn't come up with a tactful way to ask her next question, so she tossed it out, not sure if it would land with all the explosive power of a grenade or turn out to be a dud. "What about your wife?"

"Never. We never experienced The Inferno. Nor would I have ever wanted to. Not with her."

Larkin's mouth dropped open. "Wait a minute—"

He cut in with cold deliberation. "Let me make this easy for you. My wife and I were about to divorce when she died. Any version of The Inferno we might have shared was the more literal, hellish kind, not this fairy tale my family's dreamed up."

"When you say you never want to marry again . . ." she probed delicately.

"It's because I have no intention of ever experiencing that particular level of hell again."

"Okay, I understand that." Considering how well she'd known Leigh, she couldn't blame the poor man. "But that doesn't explain your need for a temporary fiancée."

"My family recently discovered Leigh and I never felt The Inferno toward each other."

Larkin was quick on the uptake. "And now they're trying to find the woman who will."

"Exactly. It's interfering with every aspect of my life. And since they won't stop until she's found, I've decided to take care of that for them."

His smile broadened. It would have turned his stunning good looks into something beyond spectacular if it hadn't been for the coldness in his green eyes. The smile stopped there, revealing a wintry barrenness that tugged at Larkin's heart. She'd always had a soft spot for strays and underdogs. In fact, some day she hoped to work full-time for an animal rescue organization. She suspected that for all his wealth and position, and despite the loving support of his large family, Rafe Dante qualified as both a stray and an underdog, which put her heart at serious risk.

"You want to pretend you've experienced this Inferno with me?" she clarified.

"In a nutshell, yes. I want all of my relatives to believe it, too. We'll become engaged, and then a few months from now, you'll decide you can't marry me. I'm sure I'll give you ample reasons for calling off our engagement. You dump me and disappear. I, of course, will be heartbroken to have found and lost my Inferno bride. Naturally, my family will be sympathetic and won't dare throw any more women my way." He smiled in satisfaction. "End of problem."

"And why won't your family throw more women your way?"

"How can they, since you were my one true soul mate?" he pointed out with ruthless logic.

"They can't have it both ways. Either you were my once-in-a-lifetime Inferno match or The Inferno isn't real. Somehow, I suspect they'll decide my one shot at Inferno happiness decided to dump me, rather than admit the family legend doesn't exist. I'll then have no other choice but to continue my poor, lonely, miserable existence never having found matrimonial bliss. A tragedy, to be sure, but I'll do my best to survive it."

Larkin shook her head in mock admiration. "A trouper to the end."

"I try."

She released her breath in a gusty sigh. "Mr. Dante—"

"Rafe."

"Rafe. There's something you should know about me. A couple of things, actually. First, I'm not a very good liar."

She opened her mouth to explain the second reason, one that would not just put a nail in the coffin of his job offer, but bury said coffin six feet down. He didn't give her the opportunity, cutting her off with calm determination.

"I noticed that about you earlier. I admire your honesty. In my opinion, it's the perfect way to convince my relatives we're in the throes of The Inferno."

Her thoughts scattered like leaves before a brisk fall wind. "Excuse me?"

"We're going to try a little experiment. If it doesn't work, we'll forget my plan and I'll find someone else. I'll still offer you a job, just a more conventional one." He eyed her with predatory intent. "But if my experiment works, you agree to my plan."

"Experiment?" she asked uneasily. "What sort of experiment?"

"First, I want to set up a few parameters."

"Parameters."

How could Leigh ever have hoped to control a man like this? Through sex, of course. But somehow Larkin suspected that would work for only so long and solely within the confines of the bedroom. She didn't need more than five minutes in Rafe's company to figure out that much about him.

"I'm a businessman, first and foremost. Before we move forward, I want to make sure we have a clear meeting of the minds."

Larkin struggled not to smile. "Why don't you explain your parameters and then we'll see what sort of agreement we can come to."

"First, I need to make it clear that this is a temporary relationship. When either of us is ready to put an end to it, it ends."

She gave it a moment's consideration before shrugging. "I suppose that's no different than a real engagement."

"Which is my next point. You don't want to lie. I don't want you to lie. So if we become engaged, from that moment forward it is real. The only difference will be at the end of the engagement—and our engagement will end—I'll see to it you receive fair compensation for your time."

"The engagement will be real, but we preplan the ending." She lifted an eyebrow. "I swear I'm not being deliberately obtuse, but I don't see how those two are mutually compatible."

He hesitated, a painful emotion rippling behind his icy restraint. "I don't do relationships well," he confessed, "or so I've been told. I suspect you'll discover that for yourself soon enough and be only too happy to end our involvement. Until then, it will be the same as any other engagement, right down to a ring on your finger and making plans for an eventual wedding day." His mouth twisted. "I'd rather it be a far distant eventual wedding day that doesn't involve actual dates and deposits."

Her sense of humor bubbled to the surface. "We don't want to rush into anything. Not after your first experience. Better to have a long engagement and make sure."

"See? You already have your lines down pat."

A matching humor lit his face and even crept into his eyes. If she hadn't been sitting, she didn't doubt for a moment her knees would have given out. He had to be one of the most stunning men she'd ever met. It didn't seem fair to have all of that rugged beauty given to one man. From high, arching cheekbones to squared chin to a mouth perfectly shaped for kissing, it didn't matter where she looked, her gaze settled on gorgeous. Even his hair was perfect, the deep brown offset by streaks of sunlit gold. But his eyes fascinated her the most, the color a sharp jade-green that seemed to darken like a shadow-draped forest depending on his mood.

"So how do we handle this?" she finally managed to ask. "Assuming I agree to your plan."

He frowned, and even that was appealing. "It may not work," he admitted. "I think we can figure that out easily enough. But you'll have to trust me."

She took a deep breath and jumped in with both feet. "Okay. What do you have in mind?" she asked.

"A simple test. If we don't pass, we scrap the idea and I'll find you a job within the organization. If it does work, we take the next step forward."

"What sort of test?" she asked warily.

"Just this."

He stood and circled the coffee table between them. Reaching her side, he held out his hand. She stood as well and took the hand he offered. Her fingers slipped across his palm. Instantly, heat exploded between them, a stunning flash that seemed to burrow into flesh and bone with unbelievable swiftness. It didn't hurt. Not precisely. It . . . melded. With a gasp of disbelief, Larkin yanked free of his touch.

"What did you just do?" they asked in unison.

Rafe took a step back and eyed her with sharp suspicion. "You felt that, too?"

"Of course." She rubbed her palm against her slacks, trying to make the sensation go away. Not that it worked. "What was it?"

"I have no idea."

She lifted her hand and stared at the palm. There weren't any marks, though based on the explosion of heat she'd experienced, it should still be smoking. "That wasn't . . . ." She cleared her throat. "That couldn't have been . . ."

She could see the emphatic denial building in his expression. At the last instant he hesitated, an almost calculating glitter dawning in his eyes. "The Inferno?" he murmured. "What the hell. Why not?"

She stared at him, stunned. "You're joking, right?" she asked.

"I don't personally believe in it, no. But I've heard The Inferno described as something along the lines of what we just felt."

"That was your test?" she demanded. "To see if we felt The Inferno when we touched?"

"No. Actually, I was going to kiss you."

She fell back another step, shocked as much by the statement as by the calm businesslike way he delivered it. "Why?"

"There's no point in becoming engaged if you aren't physically attracted to me," he explained. "My family would pick up on that in no time."

Larkin gazed at her hand and scratched her thumbnail across the faint throb centered in the middle of her palm. "So whatever just happened when we touched is just an odd coincidence?"

"I sure as hell hope so."

Huh. She lifted her head and looked at him. Their gazes clashed and the heat centered in her palm spread deeper. Hotter. Swept through her with each beat of her heart. A dangerous curiosity filled her and words tumbled from her mouth, words she'd never planned to speak. But somehow they popped out, hovering in the air between them.

"I believe you were going to kiss me," she prompted.

He approached in two swift strides. She knew what he planned, could see the intent in the hard lines of his body and determined planes of his face. He gave her ample opportunity to escape. But somehow she couldn't force herself to take the easy way out. Another personality quirk. Or flaw, depending on the circumstances. Instead, she held perfectly still and allowed him to pull her into his arms.

This was wrong on so many levels. Wrong because of Leigh. Wrong because it wasn't real. Wrong because even while she wanted to deny it, desire built within her like a tide building before a storm. Waves of it crashed over and through her until she couldn't think straight and common sense fled. He hadn't even kissed her yet, and already she could feel the helpless give of her surrender.

He leaned in and she waited breathlessly for his kiss, a kiss that didn't come. "It feels real, doesn't it?" The words washed over her like a balmy breeze, stirring the hair at her temples. "Maybe it is real. Maybe this engagement isn't such a bad idea. We can figure out what all this means."

"All what?" she managed to ask.

"All this . . ."

The kiss when it came hit with all the force of a hurricane. She didn't doubt he meant to keep it light and gentle. A tentative sampling. An initial probing. Instead, the instant he touched her, hunger slammed through her and she arched against him, winding her arms around his neck and hanging on for dear life.

It didn't surprise her in the least to discover he kissed even better than he looked. With a mouth like that, how could he not? His lips slanted across hers, hard enough to betray the edginess of his control, and yet with a passionate tenderness that had her parting for him and allowing him to sample her more fully.

All the while, he molded her against his body, the taut, masculine planes a delicious contrast to her slighter, more rounded curves. His hands swept down her spine to the base. There he hesitated before cupping her backside and fitting her more tightly between his legs. She gasped at the sheer physicality of the sensation. The scent and taste of him filled her and she shuddered, overwhelmed by sensations she'd never fully realized or explored before.

How was it possible that a simple kiss—or even a not-so-simple kiss—could have such a profound effect on her? She'd kissed any number of men. Had contemplated sleeping with a few of them. Had allowed them to touch her and had satisfied her curiosity by touching them in return. But they'd never affected her the way Rafe Dante did with just a single kiss.

Is this how it had been for Leigh?

The stray thought brought Larkin to her senses with painful swiftness. With an inarticulate murmur, she yanked free of Rafe's arms and put half the distance of the room between them. Unable to help herself, she lifted trembling fingers to her lips. They were full and damp from his kisses and seemed to pulse in tempo with the odd beat centered in her palm. She stared at Rafe. If it hadn't been for the rapid give and take of his breath, she'd have believed him unaffected.

"I think we can safely say that we're attracted to one another," she informed him.

"Hell, yes."

His voice sounded rougher than normal, low and edged with an emotion that was reflected in his eyes like green fire. He crossed to the wet bar and removed the stopper on a cut-glass decanter. Splashing some of the amber liquid into a tumbler, he glanced over his shoulder and raised an eyebrow. "Want some?"

She shook her head. She didn't dare. She'd always been a frank person. Alcohol tended to remove all caution and strip her of the ability to control her tongue. There was no telling what she'd say if she had a drink right now.

He downed the liquor in a single swallow, then turned to face her. "That was ... unexpected."

"Blame it on The Inferno," she attempted to joke.

"Oh, I intend to."

She stared at him, not quite certain of his mood. She couldn't tell if he was annoyed by what had happened, or relieved. Or maybe he just didn't give a damn. Perhaps a little of all three. Annoyed because their reaction to one another was a complication and he'd been as close to losing control of the situation as she had. Possibly even more so, since she'd been the one to finally end their embrace. Relieved because that same attraction would allow him to execute his plan. As for not giving a damn ...

No. She was wrong about that. He might hide the fact he cared, bury it deep, but she was willing to bet the Dante passion ran hotter in him than all the others.

She had a decision to make. She could turn around and walk out of the room and never return. She could tell him who she was and what she wanted. Or she could go along with his plan and see how matters developed. Every instinct warned her to get out while the going was good, or at the very least explain why this insane idea of his would never work. Maybe she'd have made the smart choice, the far less dangerous choice, if only he hadn't kissed her.

"I gather we just became engaged?" she asked lightly.

He hesitated. "Something like that."

"And will your family believe that you've gone from a total nonbeliever to an Inferno fanatic after one simple kiss?"

"Considering it happened just that way with each and every one of the Dante men in my family, yes."

"None of them believed?"

Rafe shrugged. "My cousin Marco did. He's probably the most romantic of all the Dantes."

"But not the rest of you."

"It isn't logical," he stated simply. "It's far-fetched at best and bordering on ludicrous when you look at it from a serious, rational point of view."

"I think it's sort of sweet."

His mouth curved upward. "Most women do."

A distinct awkwardness settled over her. "So, what now?"

"Now I take you home. First thing in the morning we'll get together and plan our strategy."

"Strategy." She couldn't help but laugh. "Let me guess. You're one of those organized, I-need-to-mold-the-world types, aren't you?"

"Somebody has to." He released a sigh and returned his glass to the wet bar. "Let me guess. You're one of those seat-of-the-pants, take-life-as-it-happens types?"

She wrinkled her nose. "This might be a case of opposites attract."

"Don't worry. I'll organize everything and you just go with the flow."

Her amusement grew. "Control is an illusion, you know."

He appeared every bit as amused. "Whatever you say. How about if I control us out of here and you let it happen?"

"I think I can handle that."

Larkin gathered up her purse and circled the couch toward the door. Rafe joined her, his hand coming to rest on the base of her spine in a gesture that should have been casual. Instead, it was as though he'd given her another jolt of electricity. She stumbled and her purse dropped from her hand. Turning, she could only stare helplessly at him.

"Larkin." Her name escaped on a groan and then he pulled her into his arms again.

How could something so wrong feel so right? She had no business making love to Leigh's husband. None. But she couldn't seem to resist, any more than she'd resisted his bizarre proposal. When he touched her, it all made perfect sense, probably because she couldn't think straight. All she could do was feel.

He pulled her close, so close she could hear the thunder of his heart and the rapid give and take of his breath. Or maybe she wasn't hearing his, but her own. He covered her face with kisses, swift and hungry, before finding her mouth and sinking inward. Oh, yes. This. *This* was what she craved. What she needed as desperately as sweet, life-sustaining air. Where before he'd controlled the kiss, now she took charge, giving him everything she possessed.

She heard his voice. Heard raw, guttural words. Words of want and need. And then her world tipped upside down as he swung her into his arms and carried her back to the couch. She hit the cushions with a soft bounce before he came down on top of her, his body pressing her deeper into the silken material.

"We just met," she managed to gasp.

He shifted against her, fitting them one to the other like two pieces of a puzzle. "Sometimes it's like that."

"When? With who?"

"Now. With us."

None of this made any sense. Rafe was supposed to be the rational one. The one in control. And yet, whatever had ignited between them had swept him away as completely as it had her. She wanted him with a bone-deep need that grew with each passing moment.

He made short work of the vest of her uniform, slipping buttons from their holes with a speed and efficiency that took her breath away. Parting the edges, he tackled her blouse next, button after button, before yanking the crisp black cotton from her slacks and shoving it half off her shoulders.

Rafe paused then, his hand hovering over the delicate bones of her shoulder, his dark skin tones at odds with her pale complexion. "My God," he whispered. "You're breathtaking."

No one had ever described her that way before. But seeing his stunned expression, and seeing herself through his eyes, she felt beautiful. He traced the edges of her bra, a simple, durable black cotton, sculpting the curves of her breasts. She could feel her nipples peeking through the material. An intense heat shot through her, echoed in the throbbing of her palm and sinking deep into her feminine core. "Rafe . . ."

It was her turn to touch. Her turn to explore. She cupped his face and gave in to the irresistible compulsion to trail her fingertips over those amazing planes and angles. To revel in the sheer masculine beauty of him. When she'd first seen him in the reception area, he'd appeared so self-contained, so remote. Never in a million years would she have imagined herself in this position. Who knew if the opportunity would ever present itself again? When they regained their sanity she wouldn't be the least surprised if he instituted a "no touching" rule, especially when touching was so incredibly, gloriously dangerous.

Unable to resist, she wove her fingers into his hair to anchor his head and then rose to seal his mouth with hers. He tasted beyond delicious and she couldn't get enough of him. Not his touch. Not his kisses. Not the press and drag of his body over hers.

Her hands darted to his shirt and she tugged at his tie, managing after a small struggle to rip it free from its anchor. Next, she tackled the buttons that blocked her access to the rich expanse of flesh and muscle she yearned to caress. He groaned against her mouth, levering himself upward to give her better access. Her hands hovered over his belt buckle and the bulge that lay beneath.

And that's when they heard it.

"Rafaelo?" A deep, gruff voice came from the far side of the office door, accompanied by a brisk knock. "Where are you, boy?"

Rafe swore beneath his breath. Vaulting off Larkin, he helped her to her feet. "Just a minute," he called.

She stood, swaying in place, dizzy from the swift transition from passion to normalcy. Or the attempt at normalcy. "Who's there?" she whispered.

"My grandfather Primo."

Her eyes widened in alarm and her hands shot to the buttons of her blouse at the same time his did. Fingers clashed and fumbled. She could hear the murmur of voices coming from the far side of the door. Not just his grandfather, she realized. A woman's voice, too.

"Nonna," Rafe confirmed grimly. He let her finish working on straightening her clothing while he tackled the mess she'd made of his. "My grandmother."

"Do not be ridiculous" came Primo's rumbling bass. "This is an office. It is not as though he is in a meeting, not this late. Why should I stand on the doorstep like a beggar?"

"Because he has not invited you in."

"Then I will invite myself in" was the indignant retort.

With that, he turned the knob and stepped into the room. Rafe must have anticipated his grandfather's intent because he stepped in front of her, shielding her from his grandparents' eyes while she finished buttoning her blouse and vest. Not that it really helped, considering that his shirt was open and hanging out of his trousers.

"I have been looking for you, Rafaelo," Primo announced. "I have someone I wish you to meet."

Rafe sighed as he finished making repairs to his clothes. "I don't doubt it. But it's no longer necessary."

Primo planted his fists on his waist. "Of course it is necessary. You must meet as many women as possible. How else will you find your Inferno soul mate?"

Larkin peeked out from behind Rafe's broad shoulders and saw Nonna's eyes widen with a combination of surprise and dawning comprehension. "And who is this?" she asked.

Snatching a deep breath, Larkin skirted Rafe and stepped into the light, wincing at their stunned expressions. She didn't doubt for a single moment that she looked as if she'd been doing precisely what she had been doing. Guaranteed her mouth was bare of lipstick and swollen a telltale rosy-red from Rafe's impassioned kisses. And Rafe didn't look much better, not when she compared his businesslike appearance earlier to his current rough and rumpled manifestation. And guaranteed one or both of his grandparents had caught that, and more.

Primo's gaze swept to a point midway down the line of buttons holding her vest closed and his fierce golden eyes narrowed. Either she hadn't buttoned them correctly or she'd skipped one. Maybe more than one.

Nonna, on the other hand, hovered between shock and amusement at whatever hairstyle Rafe had left in his wake when he'd plowed his fingers through the tidy little knot Larkin had fashioned at the start of her evening. She could feel part of it dangling over her left ear, while stray wisps were plastered to the right side of her face and neck.

"Hello." She gave them a wide, brilliant smile. "I'm Larkin Thatcher."

"You are with the catering service?" Primo asked, giving her clothing another assessing look.

"Not any longer. They fired me."

Apparently, they didn't know what to say to that, so she hurried to breach the silence. She couldn't help it. It was another minor personality flaw. Leigh had always called it babbling, which was a fair, if somewhat blunt, assessment.

"It was my own fault. I dropped a tray of drinks and that's a big no-no. The good news is that if I hadn't, I wouldn't have met Rafe and we wouldn't have gotten to know each other. I don't think we've finished discussing it yet. But we kind of got engaged."

Chapter Three

"Engaged," Primo and Nonna repeated in unison. Primo sounded outraged, Nonna shocked.

"Sort of." Larkin shot Rafe an apprehensive glance, as though aware that she'd jumped the gun a bit. "Or maybe not anymore. To be honest, I'm not quite sure what we are because we . . . Well, to be honest . . . Her hands fluttered over her hair and the mismatched buttons of her vest. "That is to say, we got distracted."

Beside her, Rafe groaned. "Hell."

Her gaze darted from him back to his grandparents. They didn't seem pleased with his response. "Actually, it was rather heavenly," she hastened to reassure them.

Rafe took charge of the situation. "Let's just say that the minute we touched, things got out of hand. Or in hand, depending on your viewpoint."

"The Inferno?" Primo demanded. "It has finally happened?"

Rafe hesitated. He couldn't help the hint of resistance that undoubtedly shadowed his expression. He'd experienced something when he and Larkin had first touched. But The Inferno? A connection that would last a lifetime? Sorry. Still not buying it. "Time will tell," he limited himself to saying.

To his surprise, the reluctance implicit in his tone and attitude sold the idea with impressive ease, and he couldn't help but suspect a more overt declaration would have had the opposite effect, giving his grandparents pause in the face of such a dramatic turnaround from his previous attitude.

He spared a swift glance in Larkin's direction and winced. Hell. Primo and Nonna weren't the only ones who'd picked up on his reluctance. So had Larkin. But wasn't that what they'd agreed to? Wasn't that why he'd hired her? To be his temporary fiancée? That's all it was for both of them. A transient relationship that would be nice while it lasted and, when it ended, give them both what they wanted. He'd be left the hell alone and she'd receive a nice bump to her bank account.

So why did she react as though she'd lost out on a special treat? Why that wistful look of longing, a deeply feminine look that spoke of childhood dreams and magical wishes? A look which caused him to respond on some visceral, wholly masculine level, and seemed to compel him to give her her heart's desire. Not that he could, even if he wanted to. He'd been up front with her from the start. He could never fulfill her deepest desires because he was incapable of fulfilling any woman's. The sooner Larkin accepted that, the better.

"I need to take Larkin home," he informed his grandparents. "We can discuss The Inferno once I've had time to explain it to my—" He broke off with a small smile. "My fiancée."

Primo instantly began to protest, but Nonna shushed him. "We will call tomorrow and arrange a proper meeting with Larkin," she said. "I am sure your parents would also like to meet her, yes?"

"I think we should take this slowly." Rafe stalled. "Now, if you'll excuse us?"

"First you will promise to drop her off and then leave. No more of what we interrupted here," Primo demanded. "Otherwise, you will find yourself with a wife instead of a fiancée, just like Luciano."

Rafe grimaced. Damn it. He knew that look, as well as the tone. And the reminder about his brother and Téa was a timely one. Hadn't the two of them been forced to the altar within twenty-four hours of being caught in the act? "Yes, Primo. I promise. I'll drop her off in the same condition in which I found her."

"*Era troppo poco e troppo tardi.* Too late for that, I suspect. But there will be no more..." He waved his hand to indicate Larkin's uniform. "No more button mishaps until there is a ring on her finger."

"I understand."

"And agree?" Primo shot back.

Rafe sighed. He was going to regret getting boxed in like this. "Yes. *Accosento.*"

"Very well. Take her home. Your grandmother will call in the morning to arrange a convenient time for your Larkin to meet the family."

Larkin stepped forward and held out her hand to Primo. "It was a pleasure meeting you."

"I do not shake hands with beautiful women," Primo informed her. He enfolded her in a bear hug, swamping her diminutive form, and planted a smacking kiss on each of her cheeks.

Larkin then turned to Nonna and the two women embraced. To Rafe's concern, he caught the glint of tears in Larkin's eyes and realized that she'd reached her breaking point. The events of the day must have caught up with her. First the stress of working a high-profile client, then losing her job, his proposition, followed by what had almost happened on the couch. It all added up to too much, too fast.

He didn't waste any time. Sweeping up her belongs in one hand and Larkin in the other, he ushered everyone out of the office. Not giving his grandparents time for any further questions, he wished them goodnight and urged Larkin toward the elevators. They made the ride to the subterranean parking garage in silence. But as soon as they were enclosed in his car, she swiveled in her seat to face him.

"What did your grandparents mean about Luciano? About his ending up with a wife instead of a fiancée?"

He winced at the memory. "They were caught in the act, if you know what I mean."

Larkin's eyes widened in horror. "By Primo and Nonna?" she asked faintly.

"By Téa's grandmother and three sisters. Madam is Nonna's closest friend," he explained. "When Primo heard what had happened, he stepped in and insisted Luc do the right thing."

"Meaning . . . marriage?"

Her voice had risen ever so slightly, and Rafe flashed her a look of concern. "It all worked out. They were in love. They even claim to have experienced The Inferno the first time they touched." He hadn't succeeded in reassuring her and gave it another try. "My marriage may not have been a shining example of happily-ever-after, but Luc and Téa seem genuinely in love.

Hell, for all I know, their marriage might last as long as my grandparents'."

She fell silent for a moment, which he took as a bad sign. If there was one thing he'd learned about Larkin, she didn't do silence. Sure enough, she leaped into speech. "I don't think I can do this," she announced in a rush. "I don't like deceiving people, especially people as kind as your grandparents. They take marriage and this Inferno stuff seriously."

He started the car and pulled out of his assigned parking space before replying. "That's what makes this so interesting. We're not deceiving anyone." He paused at the exit and waited for Larkin to relay her address before pulling onto the one-way street. "Admit it. We felt something when we touched."

The overhead streetlight filled the car with a flash of soft amber, giving him a glimpse of her unhappy profile. She stared down at her palm, rubbing at the center in a manner he'd seen countless times before by each and every one of his Inferno-bitten relatives.

The sight filled him with foreboding. As far as he knew, no one outside the family was aware of that intimate little gesture, one that his relatives claimed to be a side effect of that first, burning touch between Inferno soul mates. God forbid he ever felt that tantalizing itch. His palm might throb. It might prickle. That didn't mean it itched or that he'd find himself rubbing it.

"Okay, so I felt something," she murmured. "But that doesn't mean it's this family Inferno thing you have going, does it?"

"Absolutely not," Rafe stated adamantly. Though who he was so determined to convince, himself or Larkin, he couldn't say. "The point is . . . We can't rule out the possibility that it's The Inferno. Not yet. Until we do, that's what we're going to assume it is and that's what we're going to tell my family."

"And they'll believe it?" He could hear the doubt in her voice.

"Yes. Implicitly."

"But you still don't."

"I have no idea," he lied without hesitation. "It could be The Inferno. Or it could have been static electricity. Or just a weird coincidence. But telling my family that we think it might be The Inferno won't be a lie. And until we discover otherwise, we go forward with our plan."

"Your plan."

He drew to a stop at a red light and looked at her. She sat buried in shadow, her pale hair and skin cutting through the darkness while her eyes gleamed with some secret emotion. He didn't know this woman, not really. Granted, he had a mound of facts and figures, courtesy of Juice. But he hadn't yet uncovered the depth and scope of the person those dry facts and figures described. Just in the short time he'd spent with her, he'd gained an unassailable certainty that he'd find those depths to be deep and layered, the scope long-ranging and intriguing.

And he couldn't wait to start the process.

The light changed and he pulled forward. "It started out as my plan. But as soon as you told my grandparents that you were my fiancée, it became *our* plan."

"But it's a lie."

"First thing Monday I plan on putting a ring on your finger. Will it still feel like a lie when that happens?"

He heard her sharp inhalation. "A ring?"

"Of course. It's expected." He spared her a flashing grin. "In case you weren't aware, we Dantes specialize in rings, particularly engagement rings."

A hint of a smile overrode her apprehension. "I think I may have heard that about you."

"When our engagement ends, you can keep the ring as part of your compensation package."

"When," she repeated.

"It won't last, Larkin," he warned. "Whatever we felt tonight is simple desire. And simple desire disappears, given time."

"That's a rather cynical viewpoint." She made the comment in a neutral tone of voice, but he could hear the tart edge to it.

"I'm a cynical sort of guy. Blame it on the fact that I've been there, done that."

"Maybe you were doing it with the wrong woman."

"No question about that."

"Maybe with the right woman—"

"You, for instance?" He pulled to the curb in front of an aging apartment building and threw the car into Park. "Is that what you're hoping, Larkin?"

"No, of course not," she instantly denied. "I just thought . . ."

He wasn't paying her to think. He almost said the bitter words aloud, biting them back at the last instant. He wasn't normally an unkind person and she didn't deserve having him dump the remnants of his marital history on her, even if the subject of Leigh brought out the worst in him.

Nor would it pay to alienate her. Not now that he'd introduced her to his grandparents. If she chose to pack up and disappear into the night . . . He hesitated. Would it make any difference? Would his family believe he'd found his Inferno match and lost her, all in one night? Or would they think he'd concocted the story? Or worse, it hadn't been The Inferno he'd experienced, but a nasty case of lust.

No, better to stick to the plan. Better to allow his family to come to the conclusion over the next few months that he'd experienced The Inferno. Then Larkin could dump him and his family would finally, finally leave him alone to get on with his life. Until then, he would do whatever it took so his Inferno bride-to-be stuck to the game plan.

"What are you thinking?" Her soft voice broke the silence.

"Tomorrow is Saturday. Since you've been fired from your job, I assume you have the day off?"

She hesitated. "I really should be looking for a new job."

"You have a new job," he reminded her. "You're working for me now, remember?"

"A real job," she clarified.

Didn't she get it? "This is a real job and it's one that's going to take up every minute of your time, starting tomorrow."

A dingy glow from the windows of Larkin's apartment building illuminated her face, highlighting her apprehension. "What happens tomorrow?"

"I formally introduce you to some more of my family."

She shook her head. "Seriously, Rafe. I can't do this."

Without a word, he took her hand. The tingling throb surged to life, intensifying the instant their palms came into contact. "This is real. All I'm asking is for your help figuring out what it is. If my family is right and it's The Inferno, then we'll decide how to deal with it."

"And if it's not?"

He shrugged. "No harm done. Our mistake. We go our separate ways. You'll be compensated for the time I've taken away from your search for your mystery man. And I have the added benefit of being left the hell alone."

"Is that what you really want?" He could see her concern deepen. "Is that what she did to you? She turned you into the Lone Wolf the scandal sheets call you?"

"It's who I am. It's what I want." He refused to admit Leigh had played any part in his current needs. She didn't have that sort of power over him. Not anymore. "And it's what I intend to get."

Larkin gave it another moment's thought and then nodded. "Okay, I'll do it, if only to see if I can mitigate some of the damage done by your late wife." He opened his mouth to argue, but she plowed onward. "Just until we know for certain whether or not it's The Inferno."

If the only way she'd agree to his plan was by turning it into some sort of "good deed," he supposed he could live with that. And who knew? Maybe it would work. Stranger things had happened. "Fair enough." He exited the car and circled around to the passenger side. "I'll see you in."

"That's not necessary."

He waited while she climbed the steps of the front stoop and unlocked the door to the apartment building. "I insist."

He held the door open and a wide, gamine smile flashed across her face. "You think I'm going to run, don't you?"

"The thought did occur to me," he admitted.

Her smile faded. "You don't know me well enough to believe this, but I always honor my promises. Always."

"So you're finally here, Ms. Thatcher. I'd begun to think you'd skipped." The voice issued from the open doorway of the manager's apartment. A heavyset man in his sixties stood there, regarding Larkin with a stern expression, his arms folded across his chest. "Do you have your rent money?"

"Right here, Mr. Connell." Larkin dipped her hand into her pocket and pulled out the money, handing it over.

He counted it, nodded, then jerked his head toward the stairwell. "You have ten minutes to clear out."

Larkin stiffened. "Mr. Connell, I promise to pay on time from now on. I've always—"

For a split second his sternness faded. "It's not that and you know it." Then he seemed to catch himself, retreating behind a tough shell that years of management had hardened into rocklike obduracy. "You know the rules about pets. In ten minutes I'm calling animal control. And somehow I suspect they'll have questions about your *dog*."

He put an odd emphasis on the word dog, and she paled. "No problem, Mr. Connell. We'll leave immediately."

Again, Rafe gained the impression the apartment manager would have bent the rules for Larkin if it were at all possible. "San Francisco is no place to keep her, Ms. Thatcher. She needs more room."

"I'm working on it."

Rafe cleared his throat. "Perhaps a little extra rent will help clear this up. Would you consider a generous pet deposit in case of damages?" he asked.

Connell caught the underlying meaning and shot him a man-to-man look of understanding. Then he shook his head. "It isn't about the money. And it isn't about the late rent. Ms. Thatcher is as honest as the day is long." He broke off with a grimace. "At least, she is when it comes to paying her debts. The animal, on the other hand—"

"I didn't have a choice," Larkin cut in. "It was the only way to save her."

The landlord wouldn't budge. "You'll have to save her elsewhere."

"I don't suppose you could give me until the morning?"

She hadn't even finished the question before he was shaking his head again. "I'm sorry. If it were just me, sure. But others are aware of the situation, and I could lose my job if the owners found out I hadn't acted immediately once I knew about the animal."

"I understand." Rafe wasn't the least surprised at Larkin's instant capitulation. She had to possess one of the softest hearts he'd ever known. "I wouldn't want you to lose your job. It'll just take me a minute to pack."

Rafe blew out a sigh. He was going to regret this, mainly because it would make keeping his promise to Primo almost impossible. "I know a place you can stay," he offered.

Hope turned her eyes to an incandescent shade of blue. "Kiko, too?"

"Is that your dog's name?"

"Tukiko, but I call her Kiko."

"Yes, you can bring Kiko. The landlord won't object. Plus, he has a huge backyard that's dog proof."

"Really?" She struggled to blink back tears. "Thank you so much."

She turned to Connell and surprised him with a swift hug, one he accepted with an awkward pat on her back. Then she led the way upstairs. Rafe glanced around. The complex appeared shabby at best, with an underlying hint of desperation and decay. He suspected it wasn't so much that the manager was lazy or didn't care, but that he fought a losing battle with limited funds and expensive repairs.

They climbed to the third floor and down a warren of hallways to a door painted an indeterminate shade of mold-green. Larkin fished her key out of her purse and unlocked the door to a tiny single-room apartment.

"Hey, Kiko," she called softly. "I'm home. And I brought a friend, so don't be afraid."

Rafe peered into the gloomy interior. "I gather she doesn't like strangers?"

"She has reason not to."

"Abused?"

"That and more."

Rafe didn't so much hear the dog's approach, as sense it. A prickle of awareness lifted the hairs on the back of his neck. Then he caught the glint of gold as the dog's eyes reflected the light filtering in from the hallway. A low growl rumbled from the shadows.

"Kiko, stand down," Larkin said in a calm, strong voice. Instantly the dog limped forward and crouched at her feet, resting her muzzle on her front paws.

Rafe groped for a light switch, found it and flicked it on. *Son of a bitch!* This was not good. Not good at all. "What sort of dog is she?" he asked in as neutral a voice as he could manage.

"Siberian husky." Larkin made the statement in a firm, assured voice.

"And?"

"A touch of Alaskan malamute."

"And?" He eyed the animal, certain at least one of its parents howled rather than barked, ran in a pack, and mated for life.

Larkin wrapped her arms around her waist, her chin jutting out an inch. "That's it." Firm assurance had turned to fierce protectiveness overlaid with blatant lying.

"Damn it, Larkin, that's not all she is and you know it." He studied Kiko with as much wariness as she studied him. "Where the hell did you find her?"

"My grandmother rescued Kiko from a trap when she was a juvenile. But the trap had broken her leg. Gran even managed to save the leg, though it left Kiko with a permanent limp." Larkin crouched and wrapped her arms around the dog's neck. "Despite all the love and care lavished on her, it made her permanently wary of people. But she's old now. When Gran was dying, she asked me to take care of Kiko. Since Gran raised me, I wasn't about to refuse. End of discussion."

Compassion shifted across his expression. "How long ago did your grandmother die?"

"Nine months, though she was ill for about a year before that. It's been a bit of a struggle since then to keep a job while honoring my grandmother's dying wish," she found herself admitting. It had her stiffening her spine, pride riding heavy on her weary shoulders. "I've had to move around. A lot. And take on whatever jobs have come my way. But we're managing. That doesn't mean I don't have goals I hope to accomplish. I do. For instance, I'd love to work for a rescue organization that specializes in helping animals like Kiko. I just need to take care of something first."

"Finding your mystery man."

"Yes."

"Larkin—"

She cut him off. "We don't have time for this, Rafe. Mr. Connell gave me ten minutes and we've wasted at least half that already. I still need to pack."

He let it go. For now. "Where's your suitcase?"

"In the closet."

Instead of a suitcase, he found a large battered backpack and damn little else. It took all of two minutes to scoop her clothing out of the closet, as well as the warped drawers of an ancient dresser. Larkin emerged from the bathroom with her toiletries and dumped them into a small zipped section.

"What about the kitchen?" He used the term loosely, since it consisted of a minifridge, a single cupboard containing dishware for two and a hot plate.

"It came with the apartment. It'll just take me a minute to gather up Kiko's stuff and empty out the refrigerator."

She attempted to block his view of the contents, but it was difficult to conceal nearly empty shelves, especially when it took her only a single trip to the trash can to dispose of what little it contained. After she fed Kiko a combination of kibble and raw beef, she bagged up the trash and put a leash on the animal. Rafe picked up her bag. He felt a vague sense of shock that all her worldly possessions fit in a single backpack. Hell, half a backpack, since the other half contained supplies for her dog. He couldn't have fit even a tenth of what he owned in so small a space.

"You ready?" he asked.

Larkin snatched a deep breath and gave the apartment a final check before offering a resolute nod. After that it was a simple matter to lock up the apartment, turn in the keys to Mr. Connell, dispose of the trash, and exit the building. Once there, Larkin gave Kiko a few minutes to stretch her legs. Then Rafe installed the dog in the back of his car, along with the bulging backpack, while Larkin returned to her seat in the front.

"So where are we going?" she asked as he pulled away from the curb.

"My place."

She took a second to digest that. "I thought you said you knew of a place Kiko and I could stay," she said in a tight voice.

"Right. My place."

"But . . ."

He shot her a quick, hard look. "If it were just you, I could make any number of arrangements, even with it pushing midnight. But your dog—and I use the term loosely—is a deal breaker. There isn't a hotel or motel in the city that would allow Kiko through their doors. And I suspect the first place you tried would have the police coming at a dead run. Is that what you want?"

She sagged. "No," she whispered.

"Then our options are somewhat limited. As in, I can think of one option."

"Your place."

"My place," he confirmed.

Traffic was light and he pulled into his driveway a short twenty minutes later. He parked the car in the detached garage and led the way along a covered walkway to the back entrance. He entered the kitchen through a small utility room.

Larkin hovered on the doorstep. "Is it all right if Kiko comes in?"

"Of course. I told you she was welcome."

"Thanks."

The two walked side by side into the room and Rafe got his first good look at Kiko beneath the merciless blaze of the overhead lights. The "dog" was a beautiful animal, long and leggy, with a heavy gray-and-white coat, pronounced snout and a thick tail that showed a hint of curl to it—no doubt from the husky or malamute side of her family. Her golden gaze seemed to take in everything around her with a weariness that crept under his skin and into his heart. He suspected she'd have given up and surrendered to her fate, if not for her human companion.

Larkin stood at her side, dwarfed by the large animal, her fingers buried in the thick ruff at Kiko's neck. She fixed Rafe with a wary gaze identical to her dog's. "Now what?"

"What does Kiko need to be comfortable?"

"Peace and quiet and space. If she feels trapped, she'll chew through just about anything."

He winced, thinking about some of the original molding and trim work in his century-old home. "I didn't notice any damage to your apartment. I wouldn't exactly call that spacious."

"She regarded that as her de—" Larkin broke off with a cough. "Her retreat."

"Right. Tell me something, Larkin. How the hell did you smuggle her into your apartment in the first place?"

"Carefully and in the wee hours of the morning."

"I'm sure. And no one noticed her when you took her out for a walk? They never complained about her barking or howling?"

"Again, we made as many trips as possible while it was still dark. But I guess she did make noise, since we've now been kicked out." She shrugged. "It doesn't matter. Kiko isn't crazy about the city, and I wasn't planning to stay long. Just until I finished my search. Then we were going to move someplace less crowded."

"Good plan. You do realize that if anyone catches you with her, she'll most likely be put down."

"I have papers for her."

He lifted an eyebrow and waited. "You do remember that you're a lousy liar, don't you?"

For the first time a hint of amusement flickered in her gaze. "I'm working on that."

An image of his late wife flashed through his head. "Please don't. I like you much better the way you are." He gestured toward the refrigerator. "Are you hungry?"

"I'm fine."

"What about Kiko?"

"She's good until morning."

"Come on, then. There's a bedroom you can use on this level with doors that open to the backyard."

"It's fenced?"

"High and deep. My cousin Nicolò has a St. Bernard who's something of an escape artist. Brutus has personally certified my fence to be escape proof."

A swift smile came and went. "We'll see if Kiko concurs."

He could see the exhaustion lining her face, her fine-boned features pale and taut. He didn't waste any further time in conversation. Turning, he led the way toward the back of the house, throwing open the door to a suite of rooms that was at least three times the size of her apartment. She seemed to stumble slightly as she entered the room, favoring her left leg.

"You okay?" he asked.

"Oh, this?" She rubbed her thigh. "I broke my leg when I was a kid. It only bothers me when I get too tired."

"My brother Draco has a similar problem."

"I feel for him," she said, then turned in a slow circle. "Wow," she murmured. "This place is amazing."

"Nothing too good for my fiancée."

She spared him a swift, searching glance, but didn't argue. "Thank you, Rafe," she said.

He couldn't resist. He approached and tipped her face to his. From the doorway he caught a soft, warning rumble, one silenced by a swift gesture from Larkin.

"It'll take Kiko a while to realize you're safe," she explained.

His thumbs swept across the pale hollow beneath her cheekbones to pause just shy of the edges of her mouth. "Somehow I think it'll take you a while, too."

"You could be right."

He leaned down and captured her lips in a gentle caress. She moaned, the sound a mere whisper. But it conveyed so much. Hunger. Passion. Pleasure. And maybe a hint of regret. More than anything he wanted to pull her into his embrace and lose himself in her softness. She swayed against him, and it took a split second to realize her surrender came from exhaustion rather than desire.

Reluctantly he pulled back. "Wrong time, wrong place," he murmured.

She sighed. "The story of my life."

He rested his forehead against the top of her head. "I also promised Primo I wouldn't unbutton you any more tonight."

"I believe he meant from now on, not just tonight," she informed him gravely. "And I also believe you agreed to honor that promise."

He released her and took a step back, allowing them both some breathing space. "Actually, what I promised was I wouldn't unbutton you again until I put a ring on your finger." He flashed her a suggestive grin. "Come Monday, I plan to have that ring right where I need it to be. Then prepare yourself to be thoroughly unbuttoned."

Chapter Four

Larkin awoke to someone knocking on her door. Kicking off her covers, she stumbled to her feet and blinked blearily around. *What in the world?* This wasn't her shabby little apartment, but something far more sumptuous and elegant. Something a universe away from her realm of experience.

Memory crashed down around her. Getting fired. Rafe's proposal. Their shocking first touch. Their even more shocking kiss. His proposition. Her losing her apartment. And finally, her arrival here with Kiko. The knock came again and she jumped.

"Just a minute," she called.

She yanked open her bedroom door, only to discover that the knocking came from farther away. She stumbled in that direction, realizing there was someone at Rafe's front door. A very determined someone. She hovered in the foyer, debating whether or not to answer. Better not, she decided, considering it wasn't her house.

Unfortunately, the unexpected guest had a key and chose that moment to use it.

The door swung open and a woman poked her head inside. "Rafe?" She caught sight of Larkin and her eyes widened. "Oh. Oh, dear. I'm so sorry. Nonna said—"

"What is wrong, Elia?"

Larkin recognized Nonna's voice and shut her eyes. This could *not* be good.

"We've come at an inconvenient time," Elia turned to explain. "Rafe has a guest."

Nonna replied in Italian, the sound knife-edge sharp. Then the door banged open and Nonna marched into the house. "Larkin? I am surprised to find you here."

"I'm surprised to find me here, too," Larkin admitted. "In fact, I'm surprised to find us both here."

"What the hell is going on? Can't a man get a decent night's sleep?" Rafe's voice issued from on high and he appeared at the top of the staircase leading to the second story. "Mamma? Nonna? What are you doing here?"

He stood there, hands planted on his hips, his chest bare, a loose pair of sweats riding low on his hips. Larkin stared, dazzled. Despite his obvious annoyance, she'd never seen anything more gorgeous.

"Oh, my."

The comment escaped, along with her breath, her common sense, and every last brain cell she possessed. To her utter humiliation, his mother took note, suppressing a smile of amusement at her reaction.

But really... His body was an absolute work of art, sculpted with hard muscle that filled out his lean frame. His shoulders were broad, with strong, ropey arms, though she'd suspected as much when he'd lifted her in them last night and carried her to the couch in his office. His flat abdomen sported the type of six-pack she would have been only too happy to spend an entire night sampling. His mane of hair fell in rumpled abandon, the colors a lush mixture of browns and golds.

"We came over to arrange a time to meet Larkin," Elia explained. Her smile wavered. "Surprise! We met."

Rafe thrust his hands through his hair and Larkin suspected by the way his lips moved he was swearing beneath his breath. "Let me get dressed and I'll be down." His gaze sharpened, arrowing in on Larkin. "May I suggest you do likewise?"

"Oh, right." She glanced down at her own shorts and cropped T-shirt with something akin to horror before offering Rafe's mother and grandmother a weak, embarrassed smile. "Excuse me, please."

She dashed in the direction of her bedroom and closeted herself inside. Kiko stared at her alertly from where she lay in one corner, curled up on a thick, cozy rug. "What do you say we try out the backyard again and see what you think about it in the daylight," Larkin suggested.

She opened the French doors leading outside and watched while Kiko limped into the yard. She kept an eye on the dog for several minutes to assure herself the fence would withstand all escape attempts before taking a swift shower and throwing on the first set of clean clothes to come to hand. The fact that a night spent in a backpack had pressed a thousand wrinkles into them couldn't be helped.

Calling to Kiko, Larkin headed in the direction of the coffee scenting the air. She found Rafe and the women in a low, heated conversation. Since it was in Italian, she could only guess what they were saying. Nonna appeared to be offering the strongest opinion, and Larkin could make a fairly accurate guess what her opinion might be. They broke off at the sight of her and smiled in a friendly manner, though Larkin picked up on the tension that underscored their greeting.

She pretended not to notice, returning their smiles with a broad one of her own before zeroing in on Rafe. "I just want to thank you for giving me a place to stay when I lost my apartment. If you hadn't, I think Kiko and I would have been wandering the streets all night."

"What is this?" Nonna asked sharply.

"I've been trying to tell you—" Rafe began.

"No." He was cut off with an imperious wave. "I wish Larkin to tell me."

"I wasn't allowed to have a pet in my apartment building. The landlord found out about Kiko last night and kicked me out. Thank goodness Rafe insisted on walking me inside. If it hadn't been for him . . ." She shrugged. "Obviously we didn't have the time to find a place that would accept a dog, so Rafe thought the smartest option would be for Kiko and me to use his guest room for the night. I'm just relieved he has a Brutus fence." She offered a quick grin. "Turns out it's also Kiko proof."

Rafe grimaced. "After last night, I don't know whether to be disappointed or relieved."

"Last night?" Elia asked sharply.

His eyes narrowed on Kiko in open displeasure. "Full moon," he said as though that were all the explanation necessary.

"Would it be okay if I fed her now?" Larkin hastened to interrupt. "I have some kibble for her, but she needs a little bit of raw beef mixed in."

"No problem." He crossed to the refrigerator and rummaged through the contents. "Before you joined us, we were talking. Nonna and my mother would like to take you out today so you three can get to know each other."

With his head buried in the refrigerator, Larkin couldn't get a good read on either his voice or expression. "I thought I might look for a job," she temporized.

"Time enough for that on Monday." He emerged with a small packet of steak and carried it to the cutting board. "In fact, I might have something for you at Dantes."

"Oh, I don't think—"

"Perfect," Elia declared with a friendly smile. "This engagement is all so sudden it's taken my breath away."

"That makes two of us," Larkin answered with utter sincerity.

Elia's smile wavered. "Then this should give us time to catch our breath, yes?"

Larkin's gaze swiveled in Rafe's direction where he stood at the counter slicing up the raw meat. "Not unless Mr. Organize-and-Conquer plans on changing his personality by the time we get back."

The two Dante women glanced at each other and then at Larkin before breaking into huge grins of amusement. "It would seem you know my Rafaelo surprisingly well, given the short amount of time you have known him," Nonna commented.

"Perhaps that's because he doesn't bother to hide that aspect of his personality," Larkin replied.

"In case you three haven't noticed, I'm standing right here," Rafe said.

He combined Kiko's kibble with the slices of meat. The dog sat at attention, watching his every move. When he placed the food on the floor, she approached it cautiously, sniffing at the floor and around the bowl before attacking the contents.

"That's a most unusual dog you have," Elia said with a slight frown. "If I didn't know better, I'd swear she was part—"

"Definitely not," Larkin hastened to say. "She belonged to my grandmother, who raised her from the time she was a youngster."

Rafe broke in, rescuing her from any further questions. "I gather I'm Kiko's designated sitter?"

Larkin turned to him in relief. There were times his take-charge personality came in handy. This was one of them. "Do you mind?"

"Will she eat me?"

"I don't think so."

He lifted an eyebrow. "Color me reassured."

His dry tone brought a flush to her cheeks. "She's very sweet natured. Very beta."

"Well, if that's settled?" Elia asked.

Not giving Larkin a chance to come up with a reasonable excuse for avoiding their girl-bonding session, Elia urged Nonna to her feet and swept everyone toward the front door. Once there, she gave her son an affectionate kiss, one Larkin noted he returned with equal affection. Then they were out the door and tucked into Elia's car. The next instant they pulled out of Rafe's drive and headed toward the city. Larkin couldn't help tossing a swift glance over her shoulder.

Elia must have caught the look, because she chuckled. "Don't worry, Larkin. We'll return you safe and sound before you know it."

Right. It was that nerve-racking time between now and then that worried her. How in the world had she gotten herself into this mess? Yesterday she'd been free as the proverbial bird.

No entanglements. No men. Just one simple goal. Find her father.

And now . . . Larkin shot one final desperate look over her shoulder before settling in her seat. Now she had a fiancé to deal with, his family, no job, and was expected to spend the day bonding. Bonding! With Leigh's former mother-in-law, of all people. Not to mention this bizarre ache centered in her palm. She rubbed at it, which for some strange reason caused Nonna and Elia to exchange broad smiles.

Larkin sighed. What an odd family. Almost as odd as her own.

Rafe stared, thunderstruck.
"What the hell have you done to my fiancée?"

"We've been doing what women have done for centuries in order to bond," Elia said. "Shopping."

"Makeover." Nonna enunciated the word carefully, then smiled broadly, though Rafe couldn't tell if it was due to the word—one he'd never heard his grandmother utter before—or the results of said makeover. "This is something girls do together," she added with an airy gesture. "You are a man. You would not understand."

Larkin's eyes narrowed. "Don't you like it?" she asked in a neutral voice. "Your mother and grandmother went to a lot of time and expense on my behalf."

He hesitated. *Damn*. Okay, this was familiar territory. Dangerous, familiar territory. The sort of territory men discovered during their first romantic relationship. Most poor saps of his gender stumbled in unaware of the traps awaiting them until they'd fallen into the first one, impaling themselves on their own foolhardiness. Having several serious relationships plus one disastrous marriage beneath his belt, Rafe figured he'd safely skirted or uncovered all the traps out there.

Until now.

"You look lovely." And she did. Just . . . different.

Larkin's mouth compressed. *"But?"*

Behind her, Nonna and his mother also regarded him through slitted eyes and tight lips. *"But?"* they echoed.

"But nothing," he lied. Time to regain control of the situation. First item on the agenda: get rid of Larkin's backup. He gathered up his mother and grandmother and ushered them toward the door. "It's late. Nearly dinnertime. You've spent the day bonding with Larkin and I appreciate all you've done. I know this has been very sudden, and yet you've made her feel like one of the family."

"Of course we made her feel like one of us," Nonna said. "Soon she will be."

"Not too soon," he soothed. "This Inferno business is new to both of us and a bit of a shock. We need time to get to know each other before jumping into marriage."

Nonna turned on him. "Where will she stay until then?"

"Right here in my guest room."

She shook her head. "That is not proper and you know it."

He gave her his most intimidating look. Considering she was his grandmother, it met with little success. "You think I'd break my promise to Primo?"

She lifted a shoulder in a very Italian sort of shrug. "The Inferno is difficult to resist."

"If it becomes too difficult, I'll make other arrangements."

Nonna gave a dainty snort. "We will see what Primo has to say about that."

No doubt. Giving each woman a kiss, he sent them on their way before going in search of Larkin. He found her in the kitchen brewing a pot of coffee. Unable to help himself, he stood in the doorway and watched, vaguely blown away by her grace.

Her movements expressed a gentle flow, as though some inner music choreographed each step. What would it be like to dance with her? At a guess, sheer perfection. She was made to dance, and the idea of holding her in his arms while they moved together in perfect symmetry filled him with a longing he'd never experienced with or toward any other woman.

Another image formed, a picture of another sort of dance, one that also involved the two of them, but this time in bed. She had such a natural sense of rhythm, combined with a lithe, taut shape. How would she move when they made love? Would she drift the way she did now, initiating a slow, sultry beat? Or would she be fast and ferocious, pounding out a song that would leave them sweaty and exhausted?

"Coffee?"

The mundane question caught him off guard and it took him a moment to switch gears. "Thanks."

"Cream? Sugar?"

"Black."

She poured two mugs. "Do you really hate it?"

Rafe hesitated, still off-kilter. It wasn't until she ruffled her hair in a self-conscious gesture that he realized what she meant. "No, I don't hate it at all. It suits you."

And it did. Before, her hair had been long and straight, and the two times he'd seen her, she'd worn it either pulled back from her face in a braid or piled on top of her head with a clip. The stylist had cut it all off and discovered soft curls beneath the heavy weight of her hair, curls that clung to her scalp and framed her elegant features. Few women had the bone structure to get away with the stark style. She was one of them. If anything, it made her look even more like a creature from fantasy and make-believe.

"And the clothes?" she pressed.

"I suspect I'd like you better without them."

Startled, she looked at him before grinning. "There speaks a man."

"Well, yeah."

He sipped his coffee and circled her. He had to admit his mother had done a terrific job orchestrating the change. Between the haircut, the stylishly casual blouse, the three-quarter-length slacks and the scraps of heeled leather that passed for sandals, Larkin had settled on an eclectic style uniquely her own. No doubt some was due to his mother's influence. She had a knack for seeing the true nature of a person and giving them a gentle nudge in the appropriate direction, rather than simply layering on the current fashion, regardless of whether or not it suited. But the rest was all Larkin.

"How did she convince you to accept the clothes and salon treatment?"

A hint of color streaked across Larkin's cheekbones and she buried her nose in her coffee mug. "Your mother isn't an easy woman to refuse," she muttered.

"Engagement present?"

Larkin sighed. "It started out that way. Of course I said no. After all, we're not officially engaged." She set the mug on the counter with a sharp click and eyed him in open confusion. "I'm not quite sure what happened after that. All of a sudden it was a pre-engagement gift or welcome-to-the-family gift or—"

"Or a bulldozing gift."

Larkin's mouth quivered into a smile. "Exactly."

"And before you knew it, you'd had a total makeover."

"Is she always like that?"

"Pretty much. She's sort of like a tidal wave. She sweeps in, snatches up everyone in her path and carries them off. There's no resisting her. You just sort of ride the wave and hope you can slip up and over the swell before you get caught in the curl."

Larkin groaned. "I got caught in the curl. A couple curls."

He ruffled her hair. "They look good on you."

"Thanks." She picked up her mug and studied him through the steam. "Now I know where you get certain aspects of your personality. You're just like her, you know."

"Don't be ridiculous. I'm far worse."

She grinned, the tension seeping from her body. "Thanks for the warning." Kiko slipped into the room just then and came to sit at Larkin's feet, leaning against her legs. "How was she?"

He regarded the dog with a hint of satisfaction. "Let's just say, we came to terms."

Laughter brightened Larkin's eyes. "Let me guess. You gave her more steak."

He didn't bother to deny it. After all, it was the truth. "The Dantes are firm believers in bonding over food. You'll see for yourself tomorrow night."

He'd alarmed her. Not surprising, considering how much had happened in so short a time. "Tomorrow night?" she asked. "What's tomorrow night?"

"Every Sunday night the family has dinner at Primo's."

She swallowed. "The *whole* family?"

"Anyone who's available."

"And who's going to be available tomorrow night?"

"It varies week to week. We'll find out when we get there, but I'm guessing my parents, at least one of my brothers, my sister Gianna, and a couple of my cousins." She turned away, busying herself at the sink rinsing her coffee mug, but he could tell he'd upset her. Where before she was poetry in motion, now she moved in jerks and stops. "What's wrong?" he asked.

She set her cup down and turned. Turbulence dimmed her gaze and shadowed her expression. "Look. You don't know me and I don't know you. We jumped into this crazy idea without thinking it through. Everything's been moving so fast since last night we haven't even had time to discuss the details or come up with a solid game plan. I just don't think it's going to work."

"Nonna and my mother must have grilled you today."

Larkin lifted a shoulder. "Sort of."

"You must have told them something about yourself."

"Bits and pieces," she conceded.

Based on her expression, he figured she'd told them as little as she could get away with. "Clearly, nothing you said concerned or alarmed them. Stands to reason I won't be concerned or alarmed, either."

She caught her lower lip between her teeth in a gesture that was becoming familiar to him. "I didn't tell them a lot," she said, confirming his suspicion.

"Here's what I suggest. Why don't we spend tonight and tomorrow getting to know each other? If we decide it's not going to work, we'll call the entire thing off." Hell. If anything, his offer had somehow made it worse. "What now?"

"Your mother spent a fortune on my hair and clothes. I can't just leave. I owe her."

"I'll reimburse her."

Larkin's chin jerked upward. "Then I'll owe you."

"You can work it off at Dantes or we can just call it even for the time you've invested."

"I'm not a taker," she insisted fiercely.

He fought to keep his voice even. "I never said you were."

He could see the frustration eating at her. "There are things you don't know about me." She began to pace. Kiko paced with her. "I got so caught up in your job offer and then your kisses that I haven't been able to stop long enough to catch my breath. To . . . to explain things."

He zeroed in on the most interesting part of her comments, unable to suppress his curiosity. "My kisses?"

She whirled to face him. "You know what I mean. I understand that it's simple sexual chemistry, but I'm not— That is, I've never . . ." She thrust her hands through her hair, ruffling the curls into attractive disarray. "I flunked chemistry, okay?"

"Okay."

"The whole Inferno thing made me lose focus. I got off course."

Something was seriously upsetting her and his humor faded, edging toward concern. "It's not a problem, Larkin."

"It *is* a problem."

She practically yelled the words, pausing to control herself only when Kiko whimpered in distress. The dog paused between the two of them, at full alert, her ruff standing up, giving her a feral, dangerous appearance. Larkin made a quick hand gesture and the animal edged closer, rubbing up against her hip.

She forced herself to relax. "I'm sorry," she said, though Rafe couldn't tell if the apology was directed at him or the dog.

Okay, time to approach the situation the same way he did a business dilemma and apply some of his infamous Dante logic. "You told me you came to San Francisco to find someone. Is that what's upset you? You feel like this job is distracting you from finding this person?"

"Yes. No." She crouched beside Kiko and buried her face in the dog's thick coat. "My search is only one of the reasons I'm here."

"That's not a problem," he argued. "There's no reason you can't continue with your search while working for me. In fact, I might be able to help. I know someone who is excellent at finding people. He's the one who ran the security check on you last night."

"It's," she hesitated. "Complicated."

Rafe narrowed his eyes. "And you don't trust me enough to explain how or why or who."

"No," she whispered.

"Fair enough."

He approached and crouched beside her. Kiko watched him but no longer appeared distressed, and he slipped his fingers through the dog's thick fur until he'd linked his hand with Larkin's. He could feel the leap and surge of their connection the instant they touched. Though he continued to reject the possibility that it was The Inferno, he couldn't deny something bound them together, something deep and powerful and determined.

"Here's what I suggest," he said softly. "Let's do what we told my mother and Nonna we'd do. Let's take this one day at a time. We'll also give my suggestion a shot and get to know each other a little better. You tell me about yourself. Or at least, as much as you're comfortable telling me. And I'll reciprocate."

She peeked up at him. "An even swap? Story for story?"

"Sounds fair."

She considered for a minute before nodding. "Okay. Who goes first?"

"We'll flip for it. Winner's choice." He lifted an eyebrow. "Agreed?"

She considered for an instant, then nodded. "Agreed."

Satisfied to have them back on course, he released her hand and stood. "It's getting late. Why don't we throw together a simple meal, open a bottle of wine and sit outside and enjoy the evening? I think we'll find it more comfortable to reveal personal details in the dark."

"Definitely."

They worked in concert after that. He grilled up most of the portion of the steak he hadn't fed Kiko while Larkin threw together a salad. Then he nabbed a bottle of wine, a pair of glasses and a corkscrew on the way out of the kitchen. He set everything on the glass-and-redwood table on his patio. "There's some crackers in the cupboard and cheese in the fridge," he called to Larkin. "Oh, and Kiko will want the last of the beef that's in there. Middle shelf."

"She will, will she?"

"Absolutely. I'm sure that's what I heard her just say."

Larkin appeared in the doorway. "Kiko talks now?"

He lifted an eyebrow. "What? She doesn't talk to you? Ever since you left this morning, I haven't been able to get her to shut up."

To his satisfaction, the final vestiges of distress leached from Larkin's body. While she carried the last of the food to the table, he opened the cabernet and set it aside to breathe. Then he fed Kiko, who gave a contented grunt and settled down closest to where Rafe stood, no doubt hoping for another treat in the near future.

"You've corrupted her," Larkin accused. "You're going to make her fat."

"I'm trying to keep from getting eaten. There's another full moon tonight."

"She's not a wolf," Larkin muttered.

"And you're a lousy liar."

"I'll have to work on that."

"Don't." A terseness drifted through the word. "I was married to an expert, so you have no idea how much I appreciate the fact that you don't lie."

For some reason his pronouncement had the opposite effect of what he'd intended. She shot to her feet and faced him with a desperate intensity. "You're wrong. I am a liar. My being here is a lie. Our relationship is a lie. And I've told you any number of lies of omission. If you knew the truth about me, you'd throw me out right now. This minute." She shut her eyes. "Maybe you should. Maybe Kiko and I should leave before this goes any further."

Chapter Five

Larkin waited anxiously for Rafe's response. To her surprise, he didn't say a word. Instead, she heard him pour a glass of wine. The instant she opened her eyes, he handed it to her.

"I believe lying by omission is called dating," he explained gently. "No one is completely honest when they date. Otherwise no one would ever get married. All of that changes once you're foolish enough to say 'I do.'"

"Marriage equals truth time?" Is that what he'd discovered when he'd married Leigh?

"Let's just say that the mask comes off and you get to see the real person. Since we're not getting married, that shouldn't be a problem for us. Relax, Larkin. We're all entitled to our privacy and a few odd secrets."

His comments acted like a soothing balm and she sank onto her seat at the patio table, allowing herself to relax and sip the wine he'd poured. The flavor exploded on her tongue, rich and sultry, with a tantalizing after bite to it. "This is delicious."

"It is, isn't it? Primo got a couple of cases in last week and spread them out among the family to sample. It's from a Dante family vineyard in Tuscany that belongs to Primo's brother and his family."

"Huh." She went along with the drift from turbulent waters into calmer seas, even though her intense awareness of him followed her there. "And does his brother's family have that whole Inferno thing going on, too?"

"I don't know. It's never come up in discussion. Though I suspect most of the Dantes are fairly delusional when it comes to The Inferno."

Rafe settled into the seat beside her and stretched out his long legs. He was close. So deliciously close. Her body seemed to hum in reaction, flooded with a disconcerting combination of pleasure and need.

"You still don't believe it exists, despite . . ." She held out her hand, palm upward.

He hesitated, shrugged, then cut into his steak. "That's what we're going to spend the next month or so figuring out."

Careful and evasive. It would appear she wasn't the only one suffering from a case of caginess. "Are you just saying that so I'll stick with the job?" she asked, tackling her salad.

"Pretty much."

She couldn't help smiling. "Devious man."

A companionable silence fell while they ate their dinner, though she could also feel a distracting buzz of sexual awareness. It seemed to hum between them, flavoring the food and scenting the air. She forced herself to focus on the meal and the easy wash of conversation, which helped mitigate the tension to a certain extent. But there was no denying its existence or the gleam of awareness that darkened Rafe's eyes to an impenetrable forest-green. It added a unique dimension to every word and interaction, one that teetered on the edge of escalation. Or it would have if they hadn't both tiptoed around the various land mines.

After they'd finished eating, they cleared away the dishes and returned to the patio with their wine. Larkin released a sigh, half contentment, half apprehension. "Okay. Story time," she announced. "Explain to me again how this is supposed to work."

"Winner of the coin toss asks the first question. Loser answers first."

"Ouch. That could be dangerous."

"Interesting, at the very least." He tossed the coin. "Call it."

"Heads."

He showed her the coin, tails side up. He didn't hesitate. "First question. Tell me about

Kiko—and I mean the truth about Kiko. Since she's going to be around my family for the next month or two, I think I deserve the truth."

It was a reasonable question, if one she'd rather have avoided. "Fair enough. To be honest, I don't know what she is. She's definitely not pure wolf, despite her appearance. I'd guess she's probably a hybrid wolf dog." Rafe's eyebrows shot upward and Larkin hastened to add, "But I don't think she's very high-content wolf. She has too many of the traits of a dog, as well as the personality."

"Explain."

Larkin winced at the gunshot sharpness of his response and chose her words with care. "Some people breed dogs with wolves, creating hybrids. It's highly controversial. Gran was violently opposed to the practice. She considered it 'an accident waiting to happen' and unfair to both wolves and dogs, since people expect the hybrids to act like dogs." At his nod of understanding, she continued. "But how can they? They're an animal trapped between two worlds, living in a genetic jumble between domestication and wild creature. So both wolf and dog get a bad rep based on the actions of these hybrids whenever they respond to the 'wild' in their makeup."

"Got it," he said, though she could tell he wasn't thrilled with her explanation. "What about in Kiko's case? How likely is she to respond to her inner wolf?"

"She's never harmed anyone. *Ever.*" Larkin leaned on the word. "Can she? Potentially. So can a dog, for that matter. But she's more likely to run than confront, especially now that she's so old."

"How did you end up with her?"

Larkin switched her attention to the animal in question and smiled with genuine affection. Kiko lay on the patio, her aging muzzle resting on her forepaws, watching. Always watching. Alert even at this stage of her life. "We think Kiko must have been adopted by someone who either couldn't take care of her or were living someplace where they couldn't keep her because of her mixed blood. They dumped her in the woods when she was about a year old. Gran found Kiko caught in an illegal trap, half-starved."

He shot a pitying look in the dog's direction. "Poor thing. I'm amazed she let your grandmother anywhere near her."

"Gran always had a way with animals." She spared him a flashing smile. "And Kiko didn't have much fight in her by the time Gran arrived on the scene. The trap had broken Kiko's leg. She was lucky not to lose it."

"Did your grandmother set the leg herself?"

Larkin shook her head. "That would have been well beyond her expertise. She took Kiko to a vet who happened to be a close personal friend. He set the leg and advised Gran on the best way to care for Kiko. It was either that or have her put down. Since neither Gran nor I could handle that particular alternative, we kept her."

"And my family? How safe will they be with her?"

Larkin leaned forward and spoke with urgent intensity. "I promise, she won't hurt you or your family. She's very old now. The longest I've heard of these animals living is sixteen years. Most live fewer than that. Kiko's twelve or thirteen and very gentle. Except for the occasional urge to howl, she's quiet. Just be careful not to corner her so she feels trapped. Then she might turn destructive, if only in an attempt to escape what she perceives as a trap." Pleased when he nodded his acceptance, she asked a question of her own. "What about you? No dogs or cats or exotic pets?"

He shook his head. "We had dogs growing up, but I'd rather not own a pet."

She couldn't even imagine her life without a four-legged companion. "Why not?"

"You're talking about taking responsibility for a life for the next fifteen to twenty years. I'd rather not tie myself down to that sort of commitment."

It didn't take much of a leap to go from pets to a wife. If he'd thought owning a pet was an onerous commitment, how must it have felt to be married to Leigh? Larkin suspected she could sum it up in one word.

"I guess Kiko isn't the only one who doesn't like feeling trapped," Larkin murmured. "Is that what marriage felt like?" Or was it just marriage to Leigh?

"It didn't just feel that way. That's what it was." He raised his glass in a mocking salute. "One good thing came out of it. I realized I wasn't meant for marriage. I'm too independent."

That struck her as odd, considering his tight-knit family bonds. In the short time she'd known the Dantes, one aspect had become crystal clear. They were all in each other's business. Not in a bad way. They just were deeply committed to the family as a whole. And that just might explain Rafe.

"What made you so independent?" she probed. "Is it an attempt to keep your family at a distance, or something more?"

He tilted his head to one side in open consideration. "I don't feel like I need to hold my family at a distance. At least, I didn't until this whole Inferno issue came up." He frowned into his glass of wine. "I'm forced to admit they do have a tendency to meddle."

"So if it's not your family that's made you so independent, where did it come from?"

He returned his glass to the table and shook his head. "That's more than the allotted number of questions. Four or five by my reckoning. If we're playing another round, you have to answer one for me first."

"Okay, fine." She slid down in her chair and sighed. "Just make it an easy one. I'm too tired to keep all my omissions straight."

He chuckled. "Since we're not even engaged, I wouldn't want any deep, dark omissions to slip out by accident."

"You have no idea," she muttered. "Come on. Hit me. What's your question?"

"Okay, an easy one. Let's see . . . You said you broke your leg at one point. I guess that gives you something in common with Kiko."

"More than you can guess."

"So tell me. What happened?"

She tried not to flinch. She didn't like remembering that time, even though everything worked out in the long run. "I was eight. I was in a school play and I fell off the stage."

"I'm sorry." And he was. She could hear it in the jagged quality of his words. "Unless someone saw you when you were as tired as you were last night, no one would ever know. You're incredibly graceful."

"Years of dance lessons, which helped me recover faster than I would have otherwise. But I was never able to dance again." She couldn't help the wistful admission. "Not like I could before."

"Were you living with your grandmother at the time?"

"Yes." Before he could ask any more questions, express any more compassion, she set her glass on the table with unmistakable finality. "It's been a long night. I should turn in."

"Don't go."

His voice whispered into the darkness, sending a shiver through her. It was filled with a tantalizing danger—not a physical danger, but an emotional one that threatened to change her in ways she couldn't anticipate. Indelible ways from which she might never recover. She hesitated there, tempted beyond measure, despite the ghost of the woman who hovered between them. And then he took the decision from her, sweeping her out of her chair and into his arms.

"Rafe—"

"I won't break my promise to Primo. But I need to hold you. To kiss you."

A dozen short steps brought him to the French doors leading to her suite of rooms. Kiko followed, settling just outside, as though guarding this stolen time together. Even though an inky blackness enfolded the room, Rafe found the bed with unerring accuracy. He lowered her to the silken cover. A delicious weight followed, pressing her into the softness.

Despite Larkin's night blindness, her other senses came alive. She heard the give-and-take of their breath, growing in urgency. Felt her heart kicking up in tempo, knowing it beat in unison with Rafe's. Powerful hands swept over her and she caught the agitated rustle of clothing that punctuated the tide of desire rising within her. And all the while, the flare of energy centered in her palm spread heat deep into blood and bone, heart and soul.

"Are you sure this isn't breaking your promise to Primo?" she whispered.

His hand slipped around behind her and found the hooks to her bra. One quick twist and the scrap of lace loosened. He released a husky laugh. "I'd say we were teetering on a thin line."

She pulled her arms out of the sleeves of her blouse and the straps of her bra and wrapped them around his neck. "A very thin line. Maybe a kiss tonight before you leave?"

Even as the words escaped, his mouth found the joining of her neck and shoulder. Her muscles locked and her spine bowed in reaction. She'd never realized that particular juncture of her body was so sensitive. She released a frantic gasp, a small cry that held the distinct sound of a plea. How was it possible a simple touch could have such an overpowering effect? She couldn't seem to wrap her mind around it.

He cupped her breasts and drew his thumbs across the sensitive tips. Tracing, then circling, over and over until she thought she'd go crazy. He hadn't even kissed her yet, and already she was insane with a need she couldn't seem to find the words to express.

"Rafe, please."

She couldn't admit what she wanted. It was all twisted into a confused, seething jumble of conflicting urges. The urge for more. Far more. The need to stop before she lost total control. Or was it already too late for that? The sheer, unadulterated want to wallow in the heat and desire of his touch. This was wrong—not that she dared admit as much to Rafe. But she knew. And the knowledge ate at her. She shifted restlessly beneath him and he stilled her with a soothing touch.

Cupping her face, he took her mouth, obliterating the wrong beneath a kiss of absolute rightness. It was sheer perfection. Where their earlier kisses were filled with heat and demand, this one was far different. It soothed. Gentled. Offered a balm to the senses. The desperation eased, grew more languid, and she found herself relaxing into the embrace.

"You know I want to take this further," he murmured against her lips.

"You also know we can't. I couldn't look your grandparents in the face if—" She broke off with a shiver.

"Then we won't." She could hear the smile in his voice and feel it in the kisses he feathered across her mouth. "But that doesn't mean we can't come close."

She squeezed her eyes closed. "That's torture. You realize that, don't you?"

"Oh, yeah. But I can take it if you can." A warm laugh teased the darkness. "I think."

"We're playing a dangerous game."

"Do you really want me to stop?"

She considered for an entire five seconds. What had happened to her willpower? She'd never found it difficult to hold a man at arm's length. Until now. But with Rafe . . . For some reason he affected her in ways she'd never expected or experienced before. Everything about him attracted her. His looks. His intelligence. His sense of humor. His strength.

His compassion. Even his family ties—*especially* his family ties. They all appealed. And then there was her physical response to him. She'd come here wanting something specific from Rafe. What she'd gotten in its stead had been totally unexpected.

She slid her arms downward, surprised to discover that at some point his shirt had disappeared. "What if this isn't real? What if The Inferno is causing us to feel this way?"

She sensed his surprise at the question. "Is that what you think? That your response is caused by a myth?"

Larkin attempted to control her hands, but they had a mind of their own, sweeping over the sculpted muscles of his chest. He was so hard and distinctly masculine, his body so deliciously different from her own. "I've never felt like this before. I'm just trying to understand—"

"You mean rationalize what's happening." His laugh contained a wry edge. "Trust me, I understand completely. I'm not interested in another emotional entanglement. Not after Leigh."

She stilled, the reminder an icy one. "Emotional?"

He leaned in until his forehead rested against hers. "Hell, Larkin. Do you think I want this to be anything more than physical? Pure chemistry?"

"I can pretty much guess the answer to that," she said drily.

He rolled off her and onto his back, scooping her against his side. She rested her head on his shoulder and allowed her hand to drift across the flat expanse of his abdomen. He sucked in his breath, lacing her fingers with his in order to stop their restless movement. "Since the minute I met you, I've been telling myself it's a simple physical reaction. That's all I want it to be. That's all I can handle at this point in my life."

"But?"

"But then you told me about your broken leg and how you'd never been able to dance again."

"I can dance. Just not the way I did before." She shrugged. "So?"

"It just about killed me to hear you say that," he confessed roughly. "To see how it affected you."

"Is that why we ended up here?"

"Pretty much." He tugged at her short crop of curls. He blew out his breath in a sigh. "Go to sleep, Larkin."

"What about . . . ?"

"Not tonight. I'm not sure I could stop once we got started. Hell, who am I kidding? I know I won't be able to stop."

Nor would she. "Are you going to stay here with me?"

"For a while," he compromised.

She hesitated, not sure she should ask the next question. But it slipped out anyway. "What happens from this point forward?"

"I don't know," he answered honestly. "I guess we take it one day at a time."

"You think this feeling is going to dissipate over time, don't you?"

"Don't take this the wrong way, but I hope so."

"And if it doesn't?"

"We'll deal with it then."

She fell silent for a moment, then warned, "Whatever this is, Inferno or simple lust, it can't go anywhere. You aren't the only one who isn't interested in a permanent relationship."

"Then we don't have anything to worry about, do we?"

She wished that were true. But once he found out who she was, it all would change.

Rafe woke in the early hours of the morning to the haunting sound of a howl. He glanced down at the woman sprawled across him and smiled. It usually took several nights to get comfortable sleeping with a woman. But with Larkin, all the various arms and legs had sorted themselves out with surprising ease. He couldn't remember the last time he'd slept so soundly. If it hadn't been for Kiko, he doubted he'd have woken until full daylight. Speaking of which . . .

Ever so gently, he eased Larkin to one side. She murmured in protest before settling into the warm hollow left by his body, her breath sighing in pleasure. Desire coursed through him at that tiny, ultrafeminine sound. Is that what she'd do when they made love? Would she use that irresistible siren's song on him? He couldn't wait to find out.

Deliberately he turned his back on the bed and crossed to the French doors. A full moon shone down on the fenced yard, frosting the landscape in silver and charcoal. Kiko sat in the middle of the lawn, her head tipped back in a classic pose, her muzzle raised toward the moon.

She exhibited an untamed beauty that drew him on some primitive level. Part of him wanted to run, free and natural, driven by instinct rather than the intellectual side of his nature, a side he clung to with unwavering ferocity. To be part of that other world, the world that called to the untamed part of the animal before him.

Knowing he couldn't, that she couldn't, filled him with sadness. She was wildness trapped in domestication, a trap he'd do whatever it took to avoid. Before she could voice her mournful song again, he gave a soft whistle. She hesitated another moment, gave a sorrowful whine, then padded in his direction.

"It makes me so sad." Behind him, Larkin echoed his thoughts.

He turned to glance at her and froze. The moonlight bathed her nudity in silver. She stood before him, a study in ivory and charcoal. Her hair, shoulders, and breasts gleamed with a pearl-like luminescence, while shadows threw a modest veil across her abdomen and the fertile delta between her thighs. Rational thought deserted him.

She inclined her head toward Kiko. "She feels the pull of the wild, but can't respond the way she wants because she's been trapped in a nebulous existence between wolf and dog, unable to call either world her own." She fixed her pale eyes on him. "Is that how you feel? Trapped between two worlds?"

He still couldn't think straight. He understood the question, but his focus remained fixed on her. On the demands of the physical, rather than the intellect. "Larkin . . ."

She made the mistake of approaching, the moonlight merciless in stripping away even the subtle barrier of the shadows that had protected her. "Your family is such an emotional one, but you're not, are you?"

He couldn't take his eyes off her. "Don't be so sure."

A slow smile lit her face and she tilted her head to one side. With her cap of curls and delicate features, she looked like a creature of myth and magic. "So you *are* one of the emotional Dantes?"

It took him three tries before he could speak. "If I touch you again, you'll find out for yourself." The words escaped, raw and guttural. "And I'll have broken my promise to Primo."

For a long moment, time froze. Then with a tiny sigh, she stepped back, allowing the shadows to swallow her and returning to whatever fantasy world she'd escaped from. Everything that made him male urged pursuit. He knew it was the moonlight and Kiko's howling that had ripped the mask of civilization from his more primitive instincts. He fought with every ounce of control he possessed.

As though sensing how close to the edge he hovered, the dog trotted past him to the open doorway. There she sat, an impressive bulwark to invasion.

"You win this time," he told her. "But don't count on it working in the future."

With that, he turned and walked away from a craving beyond reason. And all the while he rubbed at the relentless itch centered in the palm of his hand.

She'd lost her mind. Larkin swept the sheet off the bed and wrapped herself up in its concealing cocoon. There was no other explanation. Why else would she have stripped off her few remaining clothes and walked outside like that, as naked as the day she'd been born? Never in her life had she been so blatant, so aggressive. That had been Leigh's specialty, not hers.

Leigh.

Larkin sank onto the edge of the bed and covered her face with her hands. What a fool she was, believing for even a single second she could embroil herself in the Dantes' affairs and escape unscathed. Maybe if she'd been up front with Rafe from the beginning it would have all worked out. That had been the intention when she'd asked to be assigned to the Dantes reception.

Her brow wrinkled. How had it all gone so hideously wrong? He'd touched her, that's how. He'd dropped that insane proposition on her and then before she could even draw breath or engage a single working brain cell, he'd kissed her. And she'd lost all connection with reason and common sense because of The Inferno.

The Inferno.

Larkin stared at her palm in confusion. She wanted to believe it was wishful thinking or the power of suggestion, but there was no denying the odd throb and itch of her palm. She couldn't have imagined that into existence, could she?

A soft knock sounded on her door. It could be only one person. She debated ignoring it, pretending she was asleep. But she couldn't. She crossed to the door and opened it, still wrapped in the sheet. He'd pulled on a pair of sweatpants and seemed relieved to see that she'd covered up, as well.

"It's late," she started, only to be cut off.

"I'm sorry, Larkin. Tonight was my fault." He leaned against the doorjamb and offered a wry smile. "I thought I could control what happened."

"Not so successful?"

His smile grew. "Not even a little. I can't allow it to happen again." He waited a beat. "At least, not until I have a ring on your finger."

Her eyes widened. "Excuse me?"

"Let's just say once you're wearing my engagement ring, I'll consider my promise to Primo fulfilled."

The air escaped her lungs in a rush, and she fought to breathe. "And then?" she asked faintly.

"And then we'll finish what we started tonight." He reached out and wound a ringlet around his finger. "One way or another we'll work this out." His mouth twisted. "Of course, getting whatever this is out of our systems will take a lot of work."

"What if I don't want to make love to you?"

He chuckled. The rich, husky sound had her swaying toward him. "Somehow I don't think that'll be a problem."

He leaned in and snatched a kiss, leaving her longing for more. And then he released her and left her standing there, clutching the sheet to her chest.

He was wrong. So wrong. Making love would be far more than a problem. It would be a disaster. Taking their relationship that next step would forge a deeper connection. No matter how much he wanted to deny it, it would create a bond between them that could offer nothing but pain.

Because the minute she told him Leigh was her sister—*half-sister*—and he discovered the real reason she'd approached him, he wouldn't want anything further to do with her.

Chapter Six

"*Nervous?*" Rafe asked as he downshifted the car.

They climbed farther into the hills overlooking Sausalito along a winding road that led to Primo and Nonna's. Each bend showcased breathtaking views one minute and then equally breathtaking villas the next. It was pointless to pretend she wasn't nervous, so Larkin nodded.

"A little. Your grandparents can be rather intimidating. And now there's the rest of the Dantes to contend with." She trailed off with a shrug that spoke volumes.

A far greater concern was whether any of them would somehow make some sort of quantum leap and connect her to Leigh. With such a large contingent of Dantes present for Sunday dinner, she'd be lynched for sure.

Rafe spared her a flashing smile. "Try not to worry. The intimidation factor is aimed at me, not you. I've already received a half dozen lectures from various family members who are worried about my intentions toward you. Afraid

I'll corrupt you or something." Pulling into a short drive, he crammed his car behind the ones already parked outside his grandparents' home. "Other than that, I have a terrific family."

"Big. You have a *big* family."

He glanced at her, curious. "Is it the size that worries you?"

"Everything about your family worries me," she announced ominously.

He chuckled. "Just do what I do and ignore all the drama. You don't have to answer any questions you don't want to."

"I'll tell them you said that, but somehow I doubt it'll work."

She opened the car door and climbed out, smoothing the skirt of her dress—something she rarely, if ever, wore. It was new, a purchase that both Nonna and Elia had insisted on making, despite her hesitation. In all reality, it was more of an oversize shirt than an actual dress, right down to the rolled-up sleeves and button-down collar. Unfortunately, she felt as if she'd forgotten half her outfit. Still, she couldn't deny it suited her.

A dainty gold belt cinched her waist, making it appear incredibly small, while the shirttail hem flirted in that coy no-man's-land between knee and thigh, drawing attention to her slender legs. She just hoped it didn't also draw attention to the thin network of silvery-white scars that remained a permanent reminder of her broken leg.

"Stop fussing. You look amazing." Rafe circled the car and took her hand in his. "They're all going to love you as much as Mamma and Nonna."

Despite her nervousness, she couldn't help finding the Italian inflection that rippled through his voice endearing, especially when he referred to his mother or grandmother. It was as beautiful as it was lyrical.

"I'm being ridiculous, aren't I?" She blew out a breath. "I mean, even if they don't like me it really doesn't matter. It's not like this is re—"

He stopped the words with a kiss, the unexpected power of it almost knocking her off her legs. Every last thought misted over, vanishing beneath his amazing lips. She shifted closer and wound her arms around his neck, giving herself up to the delicious heat that seemed to explode between them whenever they touched. She couldn't say how long they remained wrapped around each other, doing their level best to inhale one another. Seconds. Minutes. Hours. Time held no meaning. When he finally lifted his head, she could only stare at him, dazed. He grinned at her reaction.

"Interesting," he said. "I'll have to remember to do that anytime I want to change the subject."

"Who . . . ? Where . . . ? What . . . ? She took a tottering step backward. "Why . . . ?

His grin broadened at her helpless confusion. "You were about to say something indiscreet," he explained in a low voice. "I kissed you to shut you up. You never know who might be listening."

Larkin's brain clicked back on, along with her capacity for speech. "Got it."

It was so unfair. For her their embraces felt painfully real. But for Rafe . . . Didn't the heat they generated melt any of his icy composure? She could have sworn it did. She sighed. Maybe that was just wishful thinking on her part, which meant she was putting herself in an increasingly vulnerable position if she didn't find a way to keep her emotions in check.

"I'll be more careful from now on," she added, as much for her own benefit as for his.

She drew in a shaky breath and aimed herself toward a large wooden gate leading to the back of the house. To her profound relief, she discovered she could walk in a more or less straight line without falling down. Rafe opened the gate, and they stepped into a beautifully tended garden area filled with a rainbow of colors and a dizzying bouquet of fragrances. An array of voices greeted them, coming from the people who spilled across the lawn or sat at a wrought iron patio set beneath a huge sprawling mush oak.

The next hour proved beyond confusing as Rafe introduced her to an endless number of Dantes. Some were involved in the retail end of the Dantes jewelry empire. Others, like Rafe and his brother Luc, ran the courier service. Still others handled the day-to-day business aspects. She met Rafe's father, Alessandro, who was as easygoing as his son was intense. And she met the various wives, their radiance and undisguised happiness filling her with a wistful yearning to enjoy the sort of marital bliss they'd discovered with their spouses. Not that it would happen. At least, not with Rafe.

"Have all of the married couples experienced The Inferno?" she couldn't help but ask at one point.

Rafe gave a short laugh. "Or so they claim." She considered that with a frown, one that he intercepted. "What?"

"Well, you're the logical one, right?"

"No question."

She indicated his relatives with a wave of her hand. "And every couple here, including your parents and grandparents, claim that they've experienced The Inferno."

He shrugged. "What can I say? I've come to the conclusion that the Dante family suffers from a genetic mutation that causes mass delusion. Thank God I was spared that particular anomaly." His gaze drifted toward his younger brother and sister. "Time will tell whether Draco and Gia escaped, as well."

That earned him a swift grin. "Mutations and anomalies aside, Primo mentioned that he and Nonna have been married for more than fifty years. And I gather your parents must have been married for thirtysomething years, right?"

"Your point?"

She suppressed a wince at the crispness of his question. "Despite your unfortunate genetic anomaly, doesn't logic suggest that, based on all the marriages you've seen to date, The Inferno is real? I'd also think that the fact that you didn't experience it with Leigh and your marriage failed only adds to the body of evidence."

He didn't have a chance to answer. Draco dropped into the conversation and into the vacant chair beside them. "You're not going to convince him. Rafaelo doesn't want to believe. Plus, he's a dyed-in-the-wool cynic who isn't about to allow something as messy and unmanageable as The Inferno steal away his precious self-control."

"If you mean I refuse to be trapped in another marriage, you're right," Rafe responded in a cool voice.

Draco leaned toward her. "Oh, and did I happen to mention that he doesn't want to believe?"

Despite the pain that Rafe's comments caused, Larkin's lips quivered in amusement. "You may have said something to that effect once or twice."

"Tell me you're any different," Rafe shot back at his brother. "Are you ready to surrender your current lifestyle to the whims of The Inferno?"

Something dark and powerful rippled across the even tenor of Draco's expression. Something that hinted at the depths he concealed beneath his easygoing facade. Larkin watched in fascination. *The dragon stirs*, came the whimsical thought.

Draco took his time responding, taking the question seriously. "Answer me this. If your Inferno bride dropped into your arms out of the blue, would you push her away?"

Rafe spared Larkin a brief glance. "Is that what you think happened to us?"

"To you?" Draco seemed startled by the question. His dark gaze flashed from his brother to Larkin. "Sure, okay. Let's say it happened to the two of you. Are you going to turn away from it?"

"It didn't happen to us," Rafe stated with quiet emphasis. "It didn't because there is no such thing as The Inferno, so there's nothing to turn away from."

Draco flipped a quick, sympathetic look in Larkin's direction before responding to his brother. "In that case, either you deserve an Academy Award for your performance tonight, or you're a lying SOB. I can't help but wonder which one it is."

Rafe regarded his brother through narrowed green eyes. "You should know which one, since you're responsible for staging this little play."

"I may have orchestrated the opening scene," Draco shot right back, "but that's where my participation in this comedy of errors ended. Your role, on the other hand, appears to have taken on an unexpected twist."

Draco struck with the speed of a snake, snagging his brother's wrist. Larkin's gaze dropped to Rafe's hand and she inhaled sharply. He'd been caught red-handed—literally— rubbing the palm of his right hand with the thumb of his left, just as she'd been doing ever since they'd first touched.

"Part of the act," Rafe claimed.

But Larkin could see the lie in his eyes and hear it in his voice and feel it in the heat centered in her palm.

"Keep telling yourself that, bro, but in case you're wondering, I'm choosing Option B. That's lying SOB, in case you've forgotten." Draco deliberately changed the subject. "Hey, sister-to-be, I see I'm not the only one with an eventful childhood."

The change in subject knocked her off-kilter. "Sorry?"

He gestured to the nearly invisible network of scars along her leg. "We match. Mine was due to falling out of a tree. How about you?"

He asked the question so naturally that she didn't feel the least embarrassed or self-conscious. "Did a pirouette off a stage."

He winced. "Ouch." He nudged Rafe. "Of course, my ordeal wasn't anywhere near as bad as Rafe's."

"Rafe's?" She turned to him. "Did you break your leg, too? Why didn't you tell me?"

"I didn't break anything."

"Except a few hearts," Draco joked. "No, I meant what happened to him when I broke my leg. Didn't he tell you?"

Larkin shook her head. "No, he hasn't mentioned it."

"Oh, well, since we're all going to the lake next week, not only can he fill you in on every last gory detail, but he can show you the very spot where it went down. I'd point out the tree that started the trouble, but Rafe went crazy one year and chopped it down."

"It was infested," Rafe responded with a terrible calm. "It needed to come down before it infected other trees."

"You know, I've finally figured it out," Draco marveled. "If reality doesn't match the way you want your world to exist, you simply change your version of reality. Well, I've got news for you. That doesn't make it real. That just makes you delusional."

Larkin flinched at the word. She didn't know what had happened to Rafe all those years ago, but she could feel the waves of turbulence rolling off him, his impressive willpower all that held the emotions in check.

"I think we're being called to dinner," she said, hoping to defuse the situation. Standing, she offered her hand to Rafe. "I can't wait to sample Primo's cooking. Everyone I've spoken to has raved about it."

To her shock, he scooped her close. Lowering his head, he took her mouth in a slow, thorough kiss that caught her off guard and had her responding without thought or hesitation. "Thanks," he murmured against her lips.

"Anytime," she whispered back. Especially if it meant being rewarded with a kiss like that.

The kiss hadn't escaped the notice of Rafe's relatives, nor did she miss the gentle laughter and whispered comments that followed the two of them inside. She might have been embarrassed if not for the relieved delight on their faces. It didn't take much guesswork to understand why. Clearly, Leigh had done quite a number on Rafe and they were thankful that he'd finally put the trauma of his marriage behind him. She winced.

If they only knew.

"You didn't mention that we were expected to join your family at the lake next week," Larkin said.

"Sorry about that." He opened the door leading into the utility room off the kitchen and held it for her. "Is going to the lake with me a problem?"

With the exception of the few monosyllabic replies she'd offered in response to his various attempts at conversation, she hadn't spoken a word since they'd left Primo's. Rafe couldn't decide whether to be relieved or concerned that she'd finally started talking again. Clearly, something was eating at her. If their visit to the lake was her main concern, he could handle that and would chalk the evening up as a reasonable success. Otherwise . . .

"No. I just would have appreciated a warning."

Damn. She still wasn't looking at him, which meant her silence wasn't because of the trip to the lake. A lead-in, perhaps, or an oblique approach to the actual problem. But definitely not the problem itself. She crouched to greet Kiko, scanning the area as she did so.

"I don't see any damage in here. Maybe we should do a quick walk-through, just to be on the safe side."

"I'm sure she was fine." He stooped beside the pair and gave Kiko a thorough rub. The dog moaned in ecstasy. "Weren't you, girl?"

Sure enough, a quick inspection of the house revealed no damage. Once Larkin satisfied herself that Kiko had behaved while they were gone, he inclined his head toward the patio. "I'm not ready for the evening to end. Why don't we go outside before turning in for the night?"

She hesitated, another ominous sign. "Okay."

He removed a bottle from the refrigerator and nabbed a pair of crystal flutes, then followed her into the moonlit darkness. "Hmm. For some reason this has a familiar feel to it."

She tossed a smile over her shoulder, one filled with feminine enchantment. "Been there, done that?"

He set the bottle on the table. "Close, though a bit different from what I have planned for this evening."

She eyed the bottle and stilled. "Champagne?" A frown worried at the edges of her expression. "Are we celebrating something?"

"I guess that depends on how well this goes over." He removed a small jewelry box from his pocket and flipped it open, revealing the glittering ring within. "I couldn't wait until Monday," he explained in response to her look of shock. "Hell, I barely made it through last night."

She drew in a sharp breath. "Oh, Rafe. What have you done?"

His eyes narrowed. "You knew this was coming. I just moved up the timetable by a day or two. After last night . . ." He broke off with a shrug.

She actually blushed, which he found fascinating. At a guess, she didn't often wander around naked in the moonlight. A shame. It suited her. It also suited him.

"It's just…" She took a quick step backward. Not a good sign.

"Just what?"

He resisted the urge to follow her, stalk her. Instead, he set the ring on the table beside the bottle of champagne, realizing he'd been so focused on his own needs, he hadn't taken Larkin's into consideration. The ring and all that went with it could wait. He wanted her to enjoy their first time together, not be distracted by worries he could help ease.

"Honey, you barely spoke a word the entire way home. So either it's that, or it's the trip to the lake, or there's something else worrying you. Why don't you tell me which it is?"

He closed the distance between them and gathered her hands in his. It felt so right when he held her like this, reveling in the wash of warmth that flowed between them. Why did his family have to take something so basic, so natural, and wrap it up in myth and superstition? It was simple sexual attraction. Granted, the connection between them felt amazing. But couldn't they just call a spade a spade and let it go at that? Did they have to cloak a simple chemical reaction behind a ridiculous fairy tale?

"What's wrong, Larkin?"

Her gaze swept past him to fix on the table. "The only reason you bought me champagne and a ring is so you could make love to me."

He winced. Stripping it down to the bare-bones truth tarnished what he'd considered a romantic overture. "I thought—"

She cut him off without hesitation. "You thought that since you were buying my services, a bottle of champagne and a ring were sufficient. That you didn't have to turn it into some sort of big romantic gesture. I get that. It's not real, so why pretend it's anything more than sex, right?"

He released her hands and blew out his breath in a sigh. "Hell."

"I want to make love to you. But this—" She shivered. "An engagement ring is real, Rafe. It's a serious commitment, just like marriage. You're treating it like it's some sort of casual game or a fast, easy way to get me into bed."

Anger flashed and he struggled to contain it. "I'm well aware that marriage isn't a game. Cold, hard experience, remember?"

She stepped away from him, melting into the surrounding shadows, making it impossible to read her expression. "You hired me to do a job. You hired me to play the part of your fiancée for your friends and family and I've agreed to do that even though it goes against the grain to lie to them. You aren't paying me to sleep with you."

The comment had his anger ripping free of his control. "I'd never reduce it to something so sordid. One has nothing to do with the other. I wouldn't dream of putting a price tag on that aspect of our relationship. It would be an insult to both of us."

"And yet, you're only offering me that ring so you can get me in bed. Seems to me that's a hefty price tag."

He went after her and pulled her from the shadows and into his arms. "You know damn well why I offered you that ring. I made a promise to Primo, a promise I won't break. Do I want to make love to you? Hell, yes! But I can't and won't do it unless you're officially my fiancée. It's going to happen eventually. Why not now?" He cupped her chin, forcing her to meet his gaze. "I woke Sev this morning to open up Dante Exclusive and I picked out a ring for you. And not just any ring. A ring that reminded me of you. That seemed tailor-made for you."

He could tell his words had an impact. Her attention strayed to the table, her eyes full of curiosity and something else. A wistfulness that tore at his heart. "I won't be bought."

"And I'm not buying you. Not when it comes to this part of our relationship." His anger dampened, allowing him to rein it in. He didn't understand how she could rouse his emotions with such ease. He'd never had that problem with any other woman, not even Leigh. If anything, ice encased him whenever he'd dealt with her. "As far as I'm concerned, what happens in bed has nothing to do with your posing as my fiancée. If we'd met under different circumstances, we'd still have ended up there. You just wouldn't have had my ring on your finger."

She took a deep breath, conceding the point. "Show me the ring."

He took that as an encouraging sign. Crossing to the table, he collected the jewelry box. Removing the ring, he gathered her hand in his and slid it onto the appropriate finger. Even in the subdued lighting, the stones took on a life of their own.

The central diamond—one of the fire diamonds that made Dantes jewelry so exclusive and world renowned—sparkled with a hot blue flame. On either side of it were more fire diamonds, each subsequently smaller and bluer, the final one as pale and clear and brilliant a blue as Larkin's eyes. The stones were arranged in a delicate filigree Platinum Ice setting that seemed the perfect reflection of her appearance and personality.

"It's . . ." She broke off and cleared her throat. "It's the most beautiful ring I've ever seen."

"It's from the Dantes Eternity line."

Her gaze jerked upward. "The ones that were being showcased at the reception?"

"The very same. Every last one is unique and each has a name."

She hesitated before asking, "What's this one called?"

It was such an obvious question. He didn't understand her reluctance to ask it. But then, what he didn't understand about a woman's emotions could fill volumes. "It's called Once in a Lifetime."

"Oh. What a perfect name for it." To his concern, tears filled her eyes. "But you must see why I can't accept this."

Okay, it was confirmed. He did not—and never would—understand women. "No, I don't see. Explain it to me."

"It's Once in a Lifetime."

"I get that part." He fought for patience and tried again. "Just to clarify, you can't accept a ring from me? As in any ring? Or you can't accept this specific ring?"

A tear spilled out, just about sending him to his knees. "This one." It took her an instant to gather her self-control enough to continue. "I can't—*won't*—accept this ring."

He planted his fists on his hips. "Why the hell not?"

Now her lips and chin got into the act, quivering in a way that left him utterly helpless. "Because of the name."

"You have got to be kidding me." He snatched a deep breath, throttled back on full-bore Dante bend-'em-till-they-break tone of voice and switched to something more conciliatory. "If you don't like the name, we'll just change it. No big deal."

She shook her head, loosening another couple of tears. They seemed to sparkle on her cheeks with as much brilliance as the diamonds in the ring she couldn't/wouldn't accept. "I'm sure you can see how wrong that would be."

"No, actually I can't." He tried to speak calmly. He really did. For some reason his voice escaped closer to a roar. So much for conciliatory. "It's a prop. Part of the job. And it's yours once the job ends."

She tugged frantically at the ring. "Absolutely not. I couldn't accept it."

His back teeth locked together. "It's compensation," he gritted out. "We agreed beforehand that it would be."

Her chin jerked upward an inch. "It's excessive and taints the meaning of such a gorgeous ring." She managed to tug it off her finger and held it out to him. "I'm sorry, Rafe. I can't accept this."

Damn it to hell! "You're required to wear it as part of your official duties. Once the job ends you can keep it or not. That's up to you."

"I won't be keeping it."

He shrugged. "Then I'll give you the cash equivalent."

She caught her lower lip between her teeth in obvious agitation. "I think it's time we amended our original agreement. In fact, I insist we amend it. When you initially mentioned my keeping the ring, I didn't realize we were talking about something of this caliber."

"If I offered you anything less, my family would know our engagement isn't real."

"Which is the only reason I'm willing to wear your ring." She drew back her hand and gazed down at her palm with a hint of longing. "Maybe a different one? Something smaller. Something that doesn't have a name."

"Sev knows which ring I chose. It'll cause comment if we exchange it." He didn't give her the opportunity to dream up any more excuses. Plucking the ring from her palm, he returned it to her finger. To his relief, she left it there, though his relief was short-lived.

"About that amendment . . ." she began.

He folded his arms across his chest. He should have seen it coming. Now that she had him between a rock and a hard place, she could name her terms and he'd be forced to agree. Or so she thought. He'd soon disabuse her of that fact. Just as he had Leigh when she'd pulled a similar stunt.

"Name your demands."

Larkin blinked in surprise. "Demands?"

"That's what they are, aren't they? I've introduced you to my entire family as my fiancée. We're committed to seeing this through. And now you want to change the terms of our agreement." He shrugged. "What else am I supposed to call it?"

Everything about her shut down. Her expression. The brilliance of her gaze. Her stance. Even the way she breathed. One minute she'd been a woman of vibrancy and the next she might as well have been a wax figurine. "I don't want your money, Rafaelo Dante." Even her voice emerged without inflection. "You can keep your ring and your cash. I only want one thing. A favor."

"What favor?"

She shook her head, her features taking on a stubborn set. "When I've performed my duties to your satisfaction and the job has ended, then I'll ask you. But not before."

"I need some sort of idea what this favor is about," he argued.

"It's either something you can grant me, or not. You decide when the time comes."

He considered for a moment. "Does this have something to do with the person you're looking for?"

"Yes."

Her request didn't make the least sense. "Honey, I've already said I'd help you with that. I'm happy to help. But I hired you for a job and you deserve to be paid for that job."

She cut him off. "It's not just a matter of my giving you a name to pass on to Juice. There's more to it than that. For me, that something is of far greater value to me than your ring or cash or anything else you'd offer as compensation."

"I think I'll make that determination when the job is over. If your request doesn't strike me as a fair bargain—fair for you, I mean—then I'm going to pay you. If you don't want the ring, fine. If you don't want the money, fine. You can donate it all to charity or to the animal rescue group of your choice."

Even that offer had little impact. "Do you agree to my terms?" she pressed. "Yes or no?"

Depending on the favor, it struck him as a reasonable enough request, though he suspected he'd discover the hidden catch at some point. There had to be one. He'd learned that painful fact during his marriage, as well as from a number of the women who'd preceded his late wife. When you were an eligible Dante, it was all about what you could give a woman. Once they'd tied the knot and Leigh had dropped her sweet-and-innocent guise, she'd made that fact abundantly clear. Well, he'd deal with Larkin's hidden catch when it happened, because there wasn't a doubt in his mind that it would be a "when" rather than an "if."

"Sure," he agreed, wondering if she could hear the cynicism ripping through that single terse word. "If it's within my power to give you what you ask, I'm happy to do it."

"Time will tell," she murmured in response. "I do have one other request."

"You're pushing it, Larkin." Not that his warning had any impact whatsoever.

"It's just that I was wondering about something." She continued blithely along her path of destruction. "And I was hoping we could discuss it."

He gestured for her to finish. "Don't keep me in suspense."

"What happened at the lake when Draco broke his leg?"

"Hell. Is that what's been bothering you all night?"

"What makes you think anything was bothering me?" she asked, stung.

"Gee, I don't know. Maybe it was that long stretch of silence on the trip back from Primo's. Or the fact you've been on edge ever since our conversation with Draco."

He shouldn't have mentioned his brother. It brought her lasering back to her original question. "Seriously, Rafe. What happened to you that day at the lake? The day Draco broke his leg?"

When he remained silent, she added, "Consider it a condition of my leaving this ring on my finger."

Son of a bitch! "Now you're really pushing it."

"Tell me."

"There's not much to tell."

He crossed to the table and made short work of opening the bottle of Dom. Not that he was in the mood for a celebration. What he really wanted was to get rip-roaring drunk and consign his entire family, the bloody Inferno, and even his brand-new, ring-wearing fiancée straight to the devil. Splashing the effervescent wine into each of the two flutes, he passed one to Larkin before fortifying himself with a swallow.

"Rafe?"

"You want to know what happened? Fine. I was forgotten."

Larkin frowned. "Forgotten? I don't understand. What do you mean?"

He forced himself to make the admission calmly. Precisely. Unemotionally. All the while ignoring the tide of hot pain that flowed through him like lava. "I mean, everyone went off and left me behind and didn't realize it until the next day."

Chapter Seven

"What?" Larkin stared at Rafe in disbelief. "They left you there at the lake? Alone? Are you serious?"

Rafe smiled, but she noticed it didn't quite reach his eyes. They'd darkened to a deep, impenetrable green. "Dead serious."

"I don't understand. What happened?" she asked urgently. "How old were you?"

She could tell he didn't want to talk about it. Maybe she should have let him off the hook. But she couldn't. Something warned her that whatever had happened was a vital element in forming his present-day persona.

"I was ten and our vacation time was up, so we were getting ready to leave. My cousins and brothers and I were all running around doing our level best to pack in a final few minutes of fun while my sister Gia, chased after us, doing her level best to round us up. Since she was the youngest and only five, you can imagine how well that worked."

"And then?" Larkin prompted.

He lifted a shoulder in a casual shrug, though she suspected his attitude toward that long-ago event was anything but casual. "Draco climbed a tree in order to tease Gia. I knew it would take a while for my parents to get him down, so I took off to check on this dam I'd built along the river that fed the lake. Apparently while I was gone Draco fell out of the tree and broke his leg."

She rubbed at her own leg and winced in sympathy. "Ouch. How bad a break was it?"

"Bad. All hell broke loose. Mamma and Babbo—my mother and father—took Draco to the hospital. Gia was hysterical, so Nonna and Primo took her with them. My aunt and uncle grabbed Luc and their four boys."

He was breaking her heart. "No one wondered where you were? They just . . . *forgot* about you?"

"There were a lot of kids running around." He spoke as though from a memorized script. "They each thought someone else had taken me. Draco was in pretty bad shape, so my parents stayed overnight with him at the hospital, which is why they didn't realize I'd been overlooked."

She could sympathize with his parents' decision, having gone through a similar ordeal. Only, in her case her mother hadn't stayed with her. Gran had been the one to stick by her side day and night. "When did they figure out you were missing?"

"Late the next day. They didn't get back to the city until then. When they went to round us all up, they discovered I was nowhere to be found."

"How hideous." Larkin gnawed at her lip. "Poor Elia. She must have been frantic."

Rafe glared in exasperation. "Poor Elia? What about poor Rafe?"

"You're right." *So right.* "Poor Rafe. I'm so sorry."

He reminded her of a snarling lion, pacing off his annoyance, and she couldn't resist the urge to soothe him. She approached as cautiously as she would a wild animal. At first, she thought he'd back away. But he didn't. Nor did he encourage her, not that that stopped her.

Sliding her hands along the impressive breadth of his chest, Larkin gripped his shoulders and rose on tiptoe. His mouth hovered just within reach and she didn't hesitate. She gave him a slow, champagne-sweetened kiss. Their lips mated, fitting together as perfectly as their bodies. It had been this way from the start and she couldn't help but wonder—if circumstances had been different, would their relationship have developed into a real one?

It was a lovely dream. But that's all it was. The realization hurt more than she would have believed possible. He started to deepen the kiss, to take it to the next step. If the ring and champagne and engagement had been real, nothing would have stopped her from following him down such a tempting path. But it wasn't real and she forced herself to pull back.

She wasn't ready to go there. Not until she came to terms with the temporary nature of their relationship. Rafe might not realize it yet, but the "if" of their lovemaking would be her decision alone. The "when" on her terms.

He released a sigh. "Let me guess. More questions?"

She offered a sympathetic smile. "Afraid so."

"Get it over with."

"What in the world did you do when you returned and discovered everyone gone?" she asked, genuinely curious.

"I sat and waited for a couple of hours. After a while I got hungry, but they'd locked up the summerhouse. So I decided maybe my parents decided to punish for running off instead of staying where I'd been told and my punishment was to find my own way home."

Larkin's mouth dropped open. "Oh, my God. You didn't—"

"Hitchhike? Sure did."

"Do you have any idea how dangerous that was?" She broke off and shook her head. "Of course you do. Now."

"It all seemed very simple and logical to me. I just needed to get from the lake to San Francisco. The hardest part was walking to the freeway. And finding food."

Larkin couldn't seem to wrap her head around the story. "How? Where?"

"I came across an empty campsite." He shrugged. "The campers were probably out hiking, so I helped myself to some of their food and water."

She stared in disbelief. "You made it home, didn't you?"

"It took three days, but yes. I made it home on my own. Walked some. Snuck onto a bus at one point. The toughest part was coming up with acceptable excuses for why I was out on my own—excuses that wouldn't have the people who helped me calling the authorities."

"Your parents must have been frantic."

He crossed to the table and poured himself a second glass of champagne, topping hers off in the process. "To put it mildly."

"And ever since then?"

He studied her over the rim of the crystal flute. "Ever since then . . . what?"

She narrowed her eyes in contemplation. "Ever since then, you've been fiercely independent, determined not to depend on anyone other than yourself."

He shrugged. "It didn't change anything. I've always been the independent sort."

"Seriously, Rafe. You must have been terrified when you discovered you'd been left behind."

"Maybe a little."

"And hurt. Terribly hurt that the family you loved and trusted just up and deserted you."

"I got over it." Ice slipped into his voice. "Besides, they didn't desert me."

"But you thought they did," she persisted. "It explains a lot, you know."

"I don't like being psychoanalyzed."

"Neither do I. But at least now I understand why you hold people at an emotional distance and why you're so determined to control your world." It must have been sheer hell being married to someone like Leigh, who was a master at manipulating emotions and equally determined to be the one in control. "Did you ever tell your wife about the incident?"

"Leigh couldn't care less about my past. She pretty much lived in the now and planned for the future. Even if I had mentioned it to her, I doubt it would have made any difference."

True enough. "It makes a difference to me," Larkin murmured.

"Why?"

Because it clarified one simple fact. Their relationship would never work. His independent nature would rebel against any sort of long-term connection. Deepening that problem had been his experience at the lake all those years ago, when he'd learned to trust only himself during that three-day trek home. He wouldn't dare put his faith in someone he couldn't trust. And once he knew the truth about her, he'd never trust her. She strongly suspected once that trust was lost, it could never be regained.

She also found it interesting that he was running away from what she'd spent her entire life wishing she could have. Family. An ingrained knowledge that she belonged. Hearth and home. Though her grandmother had been a loving, generous woman, she hadn't been the most sociable person in the world. She lived on a small farm, happy with a simple, natural existence far from the nearest town. While love and obligation had kept Larkin by her grandmother's side, after her grandmother and

Leigh's death, she'd begun to long for more. The sort of "more" Rafe had rejected. During the last year of Gran's life, Larkin had created a game plan for attaining that something more. First on her agenda was to track down her father. Then she intended to obtain a job at a rescue organization and pursue her real passion— saving animals like Kiko.

The only remaining question was how to get herself out of her current predicament. Of course, she knew how. Just tell Rafe she was Leigh's sister—*half*-sister—and their temporary engagement would come to a permanent end. Then he'd either agree to what she required in lieu of payment, or he wouldn't. End of story.

She simply needed to ask how much longer he intended to drag out their engagement, and what sort of exit strategy he had planned. Knowing Rafe, he definitely had a plan.

"I have one last question," she began.

"Unfortunately for you, I'm done answering them. Guess what I want right now? I can sum it up in a single word." He set the flute on the table with enough force to make the crystal sing. He turned and regarded her with a burning gaze. "You."

How had she thought she could control this man? It would seem she was as foolish as Leigh. "I don't think—"

"I'm not asking you to think." Rafe approached, kicking a chair from his path. "I don't even care whether you choose to wear my ring or not. There's only one thing that matters. One thing that either of us wants. And it's what we've wanted from the moment we first met."

Without another word, he swept Larkin into his arms. The stars wheeled overhead as her world turned upside down. She clutched at his shoulders and held on for dear life. Her lion was loose and on a rampage and she doubted anything she said or did would change that fact.

"You're going to make love to me, aren't you?"

"Oh, yeah."

"Even though it breaks your promise to your grandfather?"

He shouldered his way into her bedroom. "I'm not breaking my promise to Primo. I put a ring on your finger. If you decide to take it off again, that's your choice. As far as I'm concerned, we're officially engaged."

"Rafe—"

He lowered her to the bed and followed her down. "Do you really want me to stop?"

The question whispered through the air, filled with temptation and allure. It was truth time. She didn't want him to stop. Just a few short days ago she'd never have believed herself capable of tumbling into bed with Leigh's husband. It was the last thing she wanted from him. But now . . .

Now she couldn't find the willpower to resist. It was wrong. So very wrong. And yet, she'd never felt anything so right. Every part of her vibrated with the sweetness of the connection that flowed between them. It danced from her body to his and back again, coiling around and through her, building with each passing second.

"I don't want you to stop," she admitted. "But I don't want you to regret this later on."

"Why would I regret it?" Despite the darkness, she could see the smile that flirted with his mouth and hear it penetrate his voice. "If anything, this should ease the tension between us."

"Or make it worse."

He leaned into her, sweeping the collar of her dress to one side and finding that sweet spot in the juncture between her neck and shoulder. "Does this feel worse?"

A soft moan escaped. "That's not what I meant."

"How about this?"

She shuddered at the caress. So soft. So teasing. Like the brush of a downy feather against her skin. "I mean when we go our separate ways. When the job ends. This will make it worse. Harder."

"It just gives us some interesting memories to take with us when we part."

"But it will end, right? You understand that?"

He traced a string of kisses down the length of her neck, pausing long enough to say, "That's supposed to be my line."

"I just want to be clear about it. That's all."

"Fine. We're both clear about it."

"There's one other thing I should tell you before we go any further."

He sat up with a sigh, allowing a rush of cool air to pour over her, chilling her. A second later the nightstand lamp snapped on, flooding the room with brightness. "The timing's wrong, isn't it?"

Larkin jackknifed upright. "No, not at all." She twisted her hands together. "Do you think you could turn off the light?"

"Why?"

"I'd just find it easier to say this next part if the light's off."

"Okay." A simple click plunged the room back into the safety of darkness. "Talk."

"I think it's only fair to warn you. What we're about to do?"

"You mean, what we were doing but aren't?"

"Oh, no. It's definitely are doing. Or rather, about to do. Unless you change your mind."

"What the hell is going on, Larkin?"

"I've never done this before, okay?" she confessed in a rush.

Dead silence greeted her confession. "You mean you've never had an affair with someone after such a short acquaintance. You've never had a one-night stand. That's what you mean, right?"

"That, too."

He swore. "You're a virgin?"

"Pretty much."

"Last time I checked, that question required a yes or no answer. It's like pregnancy. Either you are or you're not. There's no 'pretty much' or 'sort of' involved."

She blew out a sigh. "Yes, I'm a virgin. Does it really matter that much?"

"I want to say no. But I'd be lying." He stood. "Looks like Primo didn't need to make that stipulation after all. All you had to do was say three simple words and you're officially hands-off."

She couldn't let it end like this. She didn't want it to end. She'd waited all this time for the right man and despite all that stood between them, she couldn't imagine making love with anyone else. If she didn't do something to stop him, he'd leave. Who knew if she'd be given another opportunity?

Larkin didn't hesitate. Grabbing the tails of her shirtdress, she tugged it up and over her head and tossed it to one side. She fumbled for the bedside lamp and switched it on, then froze, overwhelmed by her daring.

Her actions seemed to have a similar effect on Rafe. He froze as well, staring at her with an expression that should have had her diving under the covers. Instead, it heated her blood to a near boil.

She stood before him in a silvery-blue bra and thong that were made of gossamer strands of silk, clinging to her breasts and hips like a glittering cobweb. The set was the most revealing she'd ever owned. The low-cut bra lovingly cupping her small breasts and practically serving them up for Rafe's inspection. Even more revealing was the thong. The minuscule triangle of semitransparent silk did nothing to protect her modesty. It just drew attention to her boyish hips and the feminine delta of her thighs. If she turned so much as a quarter of an inch, he'd also have a perfect view of the ripe curve of her backside.

As though he'd read her mind, he ordered, "Turn around." The demand escaped low and guttural, filled with uncompromising masculine promise. Or was it more of a threat?

She rotated in place, feeling the heat of his gaze streak across her, burning with intent. When she faced him again, he hadn't moved from his position and her nervousness increased. Why wasn't he reacting? Why hadn't he taken her into his arms and carried her back to the bed?

"Rafe?" Anxiety rippled through the word.

"Take them off. No more barriers between us."

This was not what she'd planned. "I thought you—"

He cut her off with a shake of his head. "I want you to be very certain about this. I don't want there to be any lingering questions in your mind, now or later. If you want to make love with me, if you're absolutely certain this is right for you, then take off the rest of your clothes."

The light continued to blaze across her, ruthless in slicing through the protective barrier of darkness. She understood his point. It wasn't that he didn't want to touch her. She could see the desire blazing in his expression, could feel the palpable waves of control stretched to the breaking point. Every instinct urged him to take her. To lay claim.

But he wouldn't. Not until she convinced him that she'd made this decision of her own free will, without his influencing her with one of his world-shattering kisses or beyond-delicious caresses.

She smiled.

Her hesitation dissolved. She reached behind her and unhooked the bra. The straps slid down her arms and clung for a brief instant, as did the cups. Then it drifted from her body to disappear into the pool of shadows at her feet.

A low moan escaped Rafe, and the tips of her breasts pebbled in response. "Finish it," he demanded.

She lifted an eyebrow, daring to tease. "Are you sure you wouldn't like to take care of this last part yourself?"

He took a swift step forward before catching himself. "Larkin—"

She put him out of his misery. Tiny bows held the thong in place and she tugged at them, allowing the scrap of silk to follow the same path as her bra.

"Is this enough to convince you?" She held out her hand, the one where The Inferno throbbed with such persuasive insistence. "Please, Rafe. Make love to me."

Rafe didn't need any further encouragement. In two rapid strides he reached her side and wrapped her in an unbreakable hold. Together they fell backward onto the bed. His mouth closed over Larkin's, hot with demand. She slid her fingers deep into his hair, anchoring him in place, as though afraid he'd leave her again if she didn't. Foolish of her. Now that he had her naked in his arms, he intended to keep her that way for as long as humanly possible, and hang the consequences. He only cared about making it the best possible experience for her.

"I'm feeling a bit overdressed," he murmured against her mouth.

Her laugh escaped sweet and gentle and, for some reason, drove him utterly insane. "I think I can help you with that."

She made short work of the buttons of his shirt, yanking the edges open and sliding it from his shoulders. He shrugged it the rest of the way off and sucked in his breath when her hands collided with his chest. She had a way of touching him, of stroking her fingers across him. Just. *So.* This time the strokes took her farther afield, tracing the center line of his abdomen downward until she collided with his belt.

"I can take care of that," he offered. It might kill him to let go of her even for that brief a time. But considering the rewards of stripping off his trousers, he'd manage it.

"I'd like to do it." She laughed. "At the risk of totally freaking you, I've never stripped a man before."

It didn't freak him. In fact, it had the opposite effect. He wanted her to experience it all, anything and everything she wanted. Whatever would please her. He only hoped it didn't kill him in the process.

"Tell me if I do anything that makes you uncomfortable and I'll stop."

"I don't think that'll be an issue."

He captured her hands in his before she could finish removing his clothes. "I'm serious, Larkin. It could happen. I want this to be as perfect as possible for you."

She paused in her efforts long enough to cup his face. "See, here's how I figure it. It isn't the making-love part that needs to be perfect."

Rafe choked on a laugh. "No? In that case, I've been wasting my time all these years."

"Yes, you have," she retorted. "What needs to be perfect is who you're making love with."

He closed his eyes and swallowed. Hard. "Hell, sweetheart. Don't say that. I'm not perfect."

"No, you're not." He caught the tart edge underscoring her words and couldn't help chuckling. "But in this moment, you're perfect for me. Right man. Right place. Right time."

"But no pressure."

Her laughter bubbled up to join his. "None at all."

She made short work of his remaining clothing, removing the last of the barriers separating them. He gathered her up, spreading her across the bed. Moonlight picked a path into the room through the French doors leading into the yard. It was almost as though she drew the light to her. It seemed to rejoice in her presence, gilding her with its radiance and turning her skin and hair to silver. Only her eyes retained their vibrancy, glittering a glorious turquoise-blue that rivaled the most precious gem in his family's possession.

He studied her with undisguised curiosity. Had she always been this small? This delicate? How could something so ethereal contain such a huge personality? Slowly he traced her features, finding a whimsical beauty in the arching curve of her cheekbones and straight, pert nose, her wide, sultry mouth and pointed chin. Then there was her body, superbly toned and supple.

"I don't think I've ever seen anyone more beautiful," he told her.

She shook her head. "Lots of women are more beautiful."

He stopped her denial with a slow, thorough kiss. "Not to me. Not tonight." He pulled back a few precious inches, reluctant to separate them by even that much. "Shall I prove it to you?"

Her eyes widened and she nodded, a delighted grin spreading across her mouth. "If you must."

"Oh, I must."

He cupped her breasts, their slight weight fitting comfortably in his hands. Then he bent and tasted them, one after the other, scraping his teeth across the rigid tips. Her breath escaped in a gasp and she arched beneath him, offering herself more fully. She shifted beneath him, fluid and flowing, parting her legs to accommodate him. And all the while her hands performed a tantalizing dance, tripping and teasing across him, one minute urging him onward, the next startling him with an unexpected caress.

It became a game, each trying to distract the other, their need and tension escalating with each passing moment. He discovered her legs were incredibly sensitive, and if he traced a line along the very top of her thigh and eased inward to the moist heart of her, she'd quiver like the wings of a newly hatched butterfly.

Their game came to an abrupt end when she darted downward between their bodies and cupped him, delighted by his surging response. "Larkin," he warned. "I can't wait much longer."

She squirmed in anticipation. "I don't want you to wait."

He snagged the condom he'd had the foresight to stash in her nightstand table. An instant later, he settled between her thighs. He lifted her knees, opening her for his possession. But he didn't take her immediately. Instead, he slowed, making sure that the culmination of their lovemaking would be as pleasurable as the dance that had preceded it. Gently he parted her, found the secret heart hidden within and traced the sensitive nubbin.

She shuddered in reaction, lifting herself toward his touch. He slipped a finger inward, then two, and felt the velvety contraction of impending climax. "Rafe, please," she whispered. "Make love to me."

He carefully surged forward, claiming her as his own. She reached for him and he laced her hand in his. Their palms joined, melded, just as their bodies joined, melded. Heat flashed between them, sharp and penetrating, building with each thrust of his hips.

Larkin rose to meet him, singing her siren's song, calling to him in a voice that penetrated straight to his heart, straight to his soul. It lodged there. Her sweet voice. Her heartbreaking gaze. The tempered strength of her body as it surrounded him, held him, clasped him. Refused to let him go.

Never before had he felt anything remotely similar to this. Not with any other woman. It was as though the mating of their bodies had mated every other part of them, forging a connection he'd never known existed. Heat blazed within his palm, while an undeniable knowledge blossomed.

This night had changed him and he'd never be the same again.

Chapter Eight

Larkin stirred, moaning as tender muscles protested the movement.

"You okay?" Rafe asked.

She lifted her head and forced open a single bleary eye, blinking at him. "I think that depends on your definition of 'okay.' I'm alive. Does that count?"

"It counts."

"It's the strangest sensation."

"What is?"

"Most of my body is screaming, 'Don't move.' But there are a few regions that are saying, 'Again. Now.'" She decided to experiment and shift a fraction of an inch. "I'd be an absolute fool to listen to the 'Again. Now' crowd."

"'Kay."

He started to roll off the bed and she shot out her hand to stop him. "Call me a fool."

A sleepy grin spread across Rafe's face. "Call us both fools."

She went into his arms as though she belonged, which maybe she did, despite all that stood in their way. He'd been so careful with her, so attentive, determined to make certain she enjoyed her first sexual experience. No matter what happened from this point forward, she'd always have the memory of this night to cling to.

"Thank you," she told him.

He lifted an eyebrow. "For what?"

"For being perfect. Or at least, perfect for me."

It took him a moment to reply. "You're welcome."

She lifted her mouth for his kiss, shivering as it deepened and grew more intense. Kissing she knew about. She'd kissed a fair number of men. But those experiences paled in comparison to what she shared with Rafe. With the merest brush of his lips, Rafe seduced her. That's all it took for her to want him. To feel the rising tide of desire crash over and through her. One single kiss and she knew she was meant to be his. One single kiss and she knew . . .

She loved him.

The breath caught in her throat. *No.* That wasn't possible. She pushed against his shoulders and tumbled away from him, fighting to drag air into her lungs. Sex was one thing. But love? No, no, *no!* How could she have been so foolish?

"Larkin?" He reached for her. "Sweetheart, what's wrong?"

She evaded his hand. It was *that* hand. The hand that had started all their trouble. The one that had damned her with a single touch. The touch that had infected her with The Inferno.

She snagged the sheet and wound it tightly around herself, for the first time abruptly and painfully aware of her nudity. "How are we going to get out of this?" she demanded, her voice taking on a sharp edge.

He watched her, a wary glint in his eyes. "Get out of what?"

She shook her hand at him. Sparks from the diamond ring he'd placed there sent jagged shards of fire exploding in all directions. "Get out of this. Get out of our engagement. What's your exit strategy?"

He shrugged. "I don't know. Does it matter?" He patted the mattress. "Come on back to bed. It's not like there's any hurry."

She ignored the second part of his suggestion and focused on the first. For some reason, his admission filled her with panic.

"What do you mean, you don't know? You must have a plan. You always have a plan."

He stilled, his eyes narrowing. "What's with the sudden urgency, Larkin?"

"I need to know how this is going to end. I need to know when."

He vaulted from the bed and padded across the room to where his trousers lay in a crumpled heap and snagged them off the floor. "You're having regrets."

She thrust her hand through her hair, tumbling the curls into even greater disarray. "I don't regret making love to you, if that's what you're getting at."

He grunted in disbelief. "Right."

Kicking the sheet out from beneath her feet, she came after him. "I'm serious. I don't have any regrets about that. None. Zero."

"Then what?" He tossed his trousers aside and cupped her shoulders. Dragging her into his arms, he examined her upturned face, his expression hard and remote. "One minute we were kissing and the next you're freaking out about exit strategies. What the hell happened?"

She clamped her lips shut to hold back the words. That worked for an entire twenty seconds before the truth came spilling out. "I liked it."

He stared blankly. "Liked what?"

"Making love to you."

His lips twitched and then he grinned. "That's good. I liked making love to you, too."

"No, you don't understand." She attempted to tear free of his hold, but he wouldn't let her. Why in the world had she elected to have this conversation with his stark nakedness hanging out all over the place? It made rational thought beyond impossible. "I liked making love to you. *A lot.*"

"I'm still right there with you."

She groaned in frustration. "Do I really have to spell it out for you?"

"Apparently you do."

"I liked making love with you. I *loved* making love with you. I want to do it again, as often as possible."

He reared back. "Well, hell, woman. No wonder you want to end our engagement. Who would want to make love as often as possible?"

"Stop it, Rafe." To her horror, she could feel the rush of tears. "You're supposed to be the logical one. You're supposed to have life all figured out. Hasn't it occurred to you that if we keep doing—" she shot a look of intense longing over her shoulder toward the bed "—what we've been doing, it might be sort of tough to stop?"

"Who said anything about stopping?"

Didn't he get it? "Don't you get it? That's generally what happens when engagements end. The two unengaged people stop making love." She pouted, something she hadn't done since she was all of three. "And I don't want to stop. So what happens when it's time to stop and we don't want to?"

"What usually happens is those feelings ease up or wear off." He said it so gently it made the pain all the worse. "It's just because you've never gotten to that stage of a relationship before. But trust me, I have it on good authority that excellent sex and mounds of bling aren't enough to make a woman want to stick around once she walks out the bedroom door."

That didn't make a bit of sense. "Now I don't understand." She waved her hand in a dismissive gesture when he started to explain again. "I get that you think the physical part of things will gradually grow ho-hum."

"I didn't say ho-hum," he retorted, stung.

"But what I don't get is what that has to do with the rest of it. What's bling got to do with sex, and what changes between us once we leave the bedroom? Is there a manual somewhere that explains these things? Because I have to tell you, I'm clueless."

He gave a short, hard laugh. "Are you serious? You don't know what bling has to do with sex?"

She shot him a knife-sharp look. "No. And if you do, then you've been hanging with the wrong sort of women."

He ran a hand along the nape of his neck. "I have to admit you've got me there."

"Look, I don't give a damn about bling. If the sex gets ho-hum, bling sure as hell isn't going to fix the problem, now, is it?" She planted her hands on her hips, only to make a frantic grab for the sheet when it started a southward migration. "What I need you to explain is what's going to happen after we leave the bedroom that will make our relationship turn sour?"

"I believe it has something to do with my being a loner," he explained a shade too calmly. "Too independent. Not domesticated. Emotionally distant. Intimidating."

The rapid-fire litany worried her. It sounded as if he was quoting someone, and she could take a wild stab as to the identity of that someone. "Is that what Leigh told you?" Larkin asked, outraged.

"She wasn't the only one." He scrubbed at his face, the rasp of his beard as abrasive as the conversation. "How the hell did we get on this subject anyway?"

"Let me get this straight. You think once I've gotten bored with having sex with you, I'll actually want to leave you?"

"Yes." Humor turned his eyes a brilliant shade of jade. "Though I'll do my best not to bore you while we're in bed."

"And that's your exit strategy? One day I'll be here and the next day I'll be gone and you'll tell your relatives I got bored and left."

His expression iced over. "I don't explain myself to my relatives."

She cocked an eyebrow in patent disbelief. "Something tells me you'll need to do a lot more than explain the situation to them if—*when*— I leave." He didn't argue, which told her that he privately agreed with her assessment. Sorrow filled her when she realized that even if he didn't have a plan, she did. "I'll tell you what. I'll take care of it for you."

He frowned. "You'll take care of our breakup?"

"Yes."

"And how do you intend to accomplish that?"

Stupid. Very stupid of her. She should have anticipated the question. "It's better if you don't know."

He shook his head and folded his arms across his chest. Standing there, nude and intensely male, she could see how some women might find him intimidating. Not her. She swallowed. Probably not her.

"I happen to think it's better if I do know your plan," he insisted. "Now, spill."

"If I explain beforehand, you won't be in a position to react appropriately."

"I won't let you cheat on me." The fierceness behind his comment had her stumbling back a step. "Nor will they believe you, if that's what you're going to try to tell them."

"It isn't," she instantly denied. "That never even occurred to me."

Her bewildered sincerity must have convinced him, because he nodded. "Okay, then." He throttled back a notch or two. "Give me some sort of idea so I can decide whether or not it'll work."

She didn't dare tell him, or he'd find out how well it would work right here and now. "Trust me, it'll work. Not only will they believe it, but they'll rally around you. You won't have to worry about anyone trying to find another Inferno bride for you ever again."

She looked him straight in the eye as she said it. Could he see the bleakness she felt reflected in her gaze? He must have, because he took a swift step in her direction.

"Larkin? What is it?" Concern colored his voice. "Are you ill? Is something wrong with you?"

"It's nothing like that," she assured him. Time to move this in another direction before he broke her down and forced the truth from her. She planted her splayed hands on his chest and maneuvered him backward toward the bed. "Why don't we table this discussion for now and in the meantime, I suggest you get busy and bore me."

His legs hit the edge of the mattress and he reached out to snag her around the waist as he toppled backward. She tumbled on top of him, laughing as she fell. It still hurt whenever she thought about the future. Hurt unbearably to realize this couldn't last. But she'd known it wouldn't when she'd agreed to an affair. And until the moment came when he found out who she was and what she wanted from him, she'd enjoy every single second of their time together.

Would he consider it a fair bargain? Somehow she doubted it and it distressed her to think she'd make him any more of a loner than he was already. That he'd continue to turn from people because he no longer trusted them. She'd never forgive herself if that happened. But maybe he'd understand. Maybe he'd help her and they could part on good terms.

And maybe baby pigs around the world would sprout gossamer wings and use them to fly straight to the moon.

He tunneled his fingers through her hair and thrust the wayward curls away from her face. "What are you thinking about?"

She forced out a smile. "Nothing important."

"Whatever it was, it made you look so sad."

"Then why don't you give me something else to think about?"

He didn't need any further prompting. He took her mouth in a hot, urgent kiss, one that drove every thought from her head except one. *Rafe*. The way his lips drove her wild with desire. The hard, knowing sweep of his hands across her skin. Those magical fingers that left her weeping with pleasure. It was an enchantment from which she never wanted to escape.

She gave herself up to pleasure, exploring him with an open curiosity he seemed to find intensely arousing. She'd never realized how hard and uncompromising a man's body could be in some areas and how flexible and sensitive in others. But she didn't allow a single inch of him to go uncharted.

One minute laughter reigned as she painted her way across his shape with her fingertips and the next minute it all changed. "I can't imagine ever becoming bored with you." She whispered the confession.

It took him a moment to reply. "I'm not sure it's possible for me to be bored, either. Not with you."

What should have been a light and carefree exchange took on a darker aspect, shades within shades of meaning, filled with a bittersweet yearning. She kissed him. Lingered. Then she began to paint him into her memory again. Only this time she did it with her mouth and lips and tongue, sculpting him with nibbling bites and soothing kisses. Arms. Chest. Belly. He called to her, the cry of the wolf for its mate. But all it did was drive her onward to the very source of his desire.

He didn't allow her to linger as long as she would have liked. Instead, he became the sculptor, shaping and molding her until they became one. He linked his hands with hers, just as he had before. She knew why, could see it in his eyes and in the emotions he didn't dare express. Even though he would have rejected its existence with every ounce of his intellect, it throbbed between them, giving lie to his denial.

She opened herself to him, took him deep inside her until they flowed together in perfect harmony. She wrapped herself around him, surrendering to the explosion of passion, swept away like a leaf before a whirlwind. Tumbling endlessly into the most glorious sensation, a sensation made perfect because she wasn't alone. She was there with Rafe.

The people in his life called him a lone wolf and he'd more than lived up to his reputation, to the point where he believed it himself. But there was something he'd never considered. Something he either didn't know or had forgotten. But she knew. She understood. Because she was as much a lone wolf as he was.

Wolves mate for life.

The next week proved one of the most incredible of Larkin's life. Making love to Rafe shouldn't have made such a difference. But somehow it did. Whenever she bothered to analyze the situation—which wasn't often—she realized it wasn't the sex itself that accounted for the difference, but the level of intimacy. It deepened, became richer, added a dimension to their relationship that hadn't existed before.

They spent hours in conversation, discussing every topic under the sun, except the few she avoided in order to keep him from connecting her to Leigh. Art. Science.

Literature. The jewelry business. It all became rich fodder for the hours they spent together.

How could anyone consider him emotionally distant? Or unavailable? Or even intimidating? It defied understanding. To her delight, he'd taken to Kiko, the two becoming firm friends. Even more amusing, she'd come across him a time or two conducting a lengthy one-way conversation with the animal.

"You will let me know if she answers, won't you?" Larkin teased when she discovered him discussing the merits of raw versus cooked beef with Kiko.

"I don't know what it is about that dog, but she insists on eating her food raw."

"She likes it the way nature intended. That might not be the healthiest for us, but it works for her."

He set Kiko's bowl on the ground. "Have you finished packing for the lake?"

"I have. Not that there's much to pack. Even with your mother supplementing my wardrobe, I can still fit everything into my backpack." She winced. "I think."

"Mamma does seem intent on filling your closet."

Larkin smiled, though it felt a bit forced. "Every time I go in there, I find another new outfit."

"Don't sweat it," he reassured her. "She's enjoying herself."

"I realize that." She shifted restlessly. "But it bothers me because she doesn't know our engagement is a sham. I don't want her to spend all this money on me when I'm never going to be her daughter-in-law. It's not right."

Rafe turned to face her, leaning his hip against the counter. "We've had this discussion before." He fixed her with his penetrating green gaze, his expression one that no doubt sent his employees scurrying in instant obedience. "I don't see any point in having it again."

It was the second time she'd caught a glimpse of the more intimidating aspect of his personality. Not that he hadn't warned her. She'd just been foolish enough not to believe him. She should have known better. Rafe didn't pull his punches.

"In that case, I'll wear a few of the outfits and leave the rest," she said lightly. "You can return them after I'm gone."

He shoved away from the kitchen counter and approached. "Why all this talk about leaving?"

"Well . . ." She forced herself to hold her ground even though a siren blared in her head, urging a full-scale retreat. "It occurred to me that since everyone's going to be at the lake, that might be a good time to stage our breakup."

"In front of all my relatives?"

"Bad idea?"

"Very bad idea, since I'm willing to bet the majority of them would take your side in any fight you might care to initiate."

She cleared her throat. "I wasn't thinking of a fight, so much as an announcement."

"I don't do fights or announcements. Not in public. And I sure as hell don't do them in front of my entire family."

He closed to within inches of her. No matter how hard she tried, she couldn't keep herself from falling back a pace or two. Kiko looked on with intense curiosity and Larkin suspected if it had been anyone other than Rafe proving his intimidation skills, the dog would have objected in no uncertain terms.

"Are you bored already, Larkin? Is that the problem?"

Her mouth parted in shock. "No! How could you even think such a thing?"

If shrugs could be sarcastic, Rafe had it nailed. "Oh, I don't know. Maybe it has something to do with your wanting to break off our engagement after one short week."

"In case I didn't make it clear enough last night, I'm not bored." Images of what they'd spent the time doing flashed through her head and brought a telltale blush to her cheeks. "Not even close."

"I'm relieved to hear it. But if it's not boredom . . . ?" He raised an eyebrow and waited.

Naturally, she broke first. Would she ever learn to control her tongue? "I'm afraid, okay?"

It was his turn to look shocked. "Afraid?" Shock became concern. "Of me?"

"No!" She flew into his arms, impacting with a delicious thud. "How could you even think such a thing?"

He wrapped her in a tight embrace. "Hell, sweetheart." He rested his chin on top of her head. "What else am I supposed to think?"

"Not that. Never that."

He pulled back a few inches and snagged her chin with his index finger, forcing her to look at him. "Then what are you afraid of?"

She didn't want to explain. Didn't want to tell him. But she didn't see what other choice she had. And maybe if he understood, he'd let her go before it was too late.

"It's what we were talking about before. I'm afraid to drag out our engagement," she admitted. "I'm afraid it'll hurt too much when the time comes to walk away."

Something dark and powerful moved in his gaze. How could any woman have believed for one little minute that he was emotionally distant? It wasn't distance, but self-control. Larkin had never known a man whose emotions ran deeper or more passionately than Rafe's. And because they were so strong, he'd learned to exert an iron will over them to hold them in check. Intimidating? Okay, she'd give Leigh that one. But not distant. Never that.

"I won't let you go." The words came out whisper-soft and all the more potent because of it. "I can't."

He didn't give her the opportunity to reply. Instead, he swept her into his arms. Instead of carrying her in the direction of the guest suite, he climbed the stairs to his own bedroom. They'd never made love there before and she'd understood without it ever being said that his inner sanctum was off-limits.

He lowered her to her feet once they were inside and she looked around, curious. If anything, the room confirmed her opinion of him. The furnishings were distinctly masculine, powerful and well built, with strong sweeping lines. But there was also an elegance of form and a richness of color both in the decor and the warmth of the wood accents and trim. If she'd been shown a hundred different rooms and asked which belonged to Rafe, she'd have chosen this one in an instant.

The door swung shut behind her with a loud click and she turned to discover him watching her, the intensity of his gaze eerily similar to Kiko's. "Welcome to my den," Rafe said.

She attempted a smile, with only limited success. "Am I your Little Red Riding Hood?"

He approached, yanking his shirt over his head as he came. There was something raw and elemental in the way he moved and in the manner in which he regarded her. "Not even close."

Her smile faded. The wash of emotions thickening the air between them was far too potent for levity. She responded to the scent of desire, to the perfume of want, feeling it stir her blood and feed her hunger. Her body ripened in anticipation, flowering with the need to have him on her and in her. To be possessed and to be the possessor.

"Then what am I?" she whispered.

"Don't you know?" He backed her toward the bed. "Haven't you figured it out yet?"

In that instant she understood. Knew what he was to her and she to him.

She was his mate.

She could see it in his stance and in the possessiveness of his gaze, in the timbre of his voice and the strength of his desire. By bringing her here, he'd lowered his guard and allowed her into the most private part of his home. And into the most private part of himself.

Even as she surrendered to his touch, a part of her wept. He'd finally opened himself to her, and in a few short weeks—possibly in just days— she was going to destroy not just his trust, but any hope of his ever loving her.

Chapter Nine

The closer they came to the lake house over the course of the three hour drive, the more Larkin's tension increased. Rafe could feel it pouring off her in waves. It didn't take a genius to guess the cause.

"No one's going to know," he told her.

She tilted her head to one side and peered at him over a spare set of his sunglasses, since she didn't own a pair of her own. "They're not going to know that we're sleeping together? Or they're not going to know that our engagement is a sham?"

His mouth twitched in amusement at the way the glasses swamped her delicate features. "Yes."

She considered that for a moment before releasing a low, husky laugh. "You're right. Blame it on sheer unadulterated guilt."

"Guilt because you're sleeping with me, or guilt because our engagement's a sham?"

She shot him a swift grin. "Yes."

"Let's take care of your first concern." He spared her a heated look. "Sex."

"I believe you take care of that on a regular basis," she responded promptly.

"I do my best," he replied with impressive modesty. "Fortunately for you, you're about to discover that the engagement ring you're wearing is magical."

She held it out, admiring the way it caught and refracted the light. "It is?"

"Without question. The minute I put it on your finger, it created a net of blissful ignorance."

"Funny. I don't feel blissfully ignorant."

He snorted. "Not you. My family."

"Ah." To his relief, she began to relax. "And I assume this magical net keeps everyone from knowing we're sleeping together?"

"Without question. They may suspect, but the ring will cause them to turn a blind eye to it."

"Even Primo and Nonna?"

"Especially Primo and Nonna," he confirmed.

"And my other concern?"

That eventuality continued to hover between them like a malevolent cloud. "The reality—or lack thereof—of our engagement is also a nonissue."

"And why is that?" she asked.

He could hear the intense curiosity in her voice, along with a yearning that he found quite satisfying. "I have a plan."

"Which is?" she asked uneasily.

He debated for a moment. "I don't think I'm going to tell you. Not yet." At least not until he figured out how to convince her it would work. It would be a huge step for both of them. Only time could prove whether that step was the right one. "My plan needs a while to ripen."

She shifted in her seat, betraying her nervousness. "You do remember that I also have a plan, right?"

"We'll consider that plan B."

"I'm not sure that'll work," she murmured.

"Why not?"

She released a sigh filled with regret. "It's sort of on automatic. Eventually it's going to go off by itself."

What the hell did that mean? "What the hell does that mean?"

But they arrived at the lake before she responded, which caused her as much relief as it caused him annoyance. He filed the information away for a more opportune time to drag out the details. One nice thing about his fiancée was that she found it impossible to keep secrets from him. A single, tiny nudge and it all spilled out.

They pulled up to the main residence, a huge sprawling building. When he'd been a kid, the place had looked far different, more rustic. But in recent years the family had rebuilt and expanded it, cantilevering the newer two wings out over the lake. They'd also added private cabins, which dotted the shoreline and were better suited for the privacy issues of newly married couples.

Larkin leaned forward, her breath catching. "My God, it's magnificent."

He smiled in satisfaction. "Maybe you can understand why we all make the effort to come here each year."

"I'd never want to leave."

He parked in the gravel area adjacent to the storage shed and workshop. "We'll be expected to stay at the main house."

"In separate rooms, I assume."

"Guaranteed. Don't let it worry you. I know plenty of places where we can find some privacy."

She appeared intrigued by the possibility. "I've never made love in the woods before."

"Only because there hasn't been the opportunity until now. I look forward to correcting the oversight."

She shot him a mischievous look. "So do I."

The next several days proved enlightening. After an initial shyness, both Larkin and Kiko took to his family with impressive enthusiasm. It made him realize she never talked about her family, other than the occasional reference to her grandmother, and he couldn't help but wonder why.

Where he had always found his family somewhat intrusive, particularly when it came to certain personal issues such as women and romance, Larkin soaked in the love and attention as though it were a new and wondrous experience. Over the days they spent at the lake, he noted she blossomed the most beneath the attention of his mother and father and he remembered her mentioning she'd been brought up by her grandmother. She'd always taken pains to change the subject whenever the conversation turned to the topic of her parents, which raised an interesting question. What had happened to them?

Toward the end of their stay, he finally found a private moment to ask. He'd arranged for a picnic lunch he'd set up on one of the rafts dotting the lake, this one offering the most privacy from curious eyes. She laughed in surprised delight when they swam out to the raft and discovered lunch waiting for them.

"What have you been up to, Rafaelo Dante?" She knelt on the raft and opened the lid of the basket, peering inside. Freezer packs kept the chicken and Primo's uniquely spiced potato salad icy cold, as well as the bottle of white wine Rafe had tossed in at the last minute. She rocked back on her heels. "This is . . ." She shook her head, struggling to speak. "This is *amazing*."

Something in her voice alerted him and he took her chin in his hand and tilted her face toward him. Sure enough, he caught the telltale glint of tears. "What's wrong?"

"Nothing's wrong," she instantly denied. "It's just . . ." She gazed out across the lake, emotions darting across her face, one after another. Longing. Sorrow. Regret. Then they vanished, replaced by a grateful smile. "Thank you for bringing me here. This week has been like some sort of beautiful dream. I've enjoyed every minute of my time here."

"I gather the ring is working? No one's given you any trouble?"

She stared down at it in open pleasure. "Your family hasn't given me a moment's trouble. And they were all so excited to see me wearing it." Then the sorrow and regret returned. "I hope they won't be too crushed when our engagement ends."

Time for the first step of his plan. "There's no rush to end it," he remarked in an offhand manner. "In fact, I think it may be necessary to continue the engagement for a while longer. Would that be a problem?"

A tiny frown creased her brow. "I—I'm not sure."

He didn't give her a chance to invent a list of excuses. No doubt she'd come up with them, but he had a plan for that, too. Hoping to distract her, he filled their plates with food. Then he opened the wine and poured them each a glass.

They sat in companionable silence, soaking up the August sun while they ate and sipped their wine. It gave him plenty of opportunity to admire the sleek red one-piece she wore and the way it showcased her subtle curves. She was beautifully proportioned. Magnificent legs. A backside with just the perfect amount of curve to it. Narrow hips and an even narrower waist. And her breasts, outlined in the thin Lycra of her swimsuit, were the most delectable he'd ever seen. A dessert he planned to savor at the earliest possible opportunity.

"Tell me something, Larkin."

"Hmm?"

He gathered up their empty plates, slipped them into a plastic bag and returned them to the basket. "Why were you raised by your grandmother? What happened to your parents?"

The instant his question penetrated, she stilled. It was like watching a wild animal who'd caught the unexpected scent of a predator. She didn't say anything for a long time, which was so out of character for her that he knew he'd stumbled onto something important. She pulled her legs against her chest and wrapped her arms around them, her grip on the stem of her wineglass so tight it was a wonder it didn't shatter.

She remained silent for long minutes, staring toward shore where Kiko chased a flutter of butterflies. "Gran raised me because my mother didn't want me."

"What?" It was so contrary to his way of thinking, he struggled to process it. "How could someone not want you?"

She buried her nose in her wineglass. "I don't like to discuss it."

She didn't actually use the words "I don't like to discuss it *with strangers,*" but she might as well have. If anything, it made him all the more determined to pry it out of her. Hadn't she done the same for him when it came to his relationship with Leigh, as well as those long-ago events at the lake when Draco had broken his leg? He understood all too well what it felt like to have a poison eating away inside. Larkin had lanced his wound. It was only fair he do the same for her.

"What about your father?"

She shifted. "He wasn't in the picture."

"He left your mother?"

To his relief, Larkin allowed the question, even smiled at it. "My mother wasn't the sort of woman you leave. Not if you're a typical red-blooded male. No, she left my father to return to her husband."

He couldn't hide how appalled he was, couldn't even keep it from bleeding into his voice. "That's how you ended up living with your grandmother?"

Larkin nodded. "My mother discovered she was pregnant with me shortly after she returned home. She and her husband already had a daughter, a legitimate one. Naturally, he wasn't about to have proof of her infidelity hanging around the house, or have my presence contaminating his own daughter. So Mother kept my half-sister and turned me over to Gran. She even gave me her maiden name, so her husband wouldn't have any connection to me. Considering some of the alternatives, it wasn't such a bad option."

In other words, her mother had abandoned her. He swore, a word that caused her to flinch in reaction. "And your father? What happened to him?"

She didn't reply. Instead she lifted a shoulder in an offhand shrug and held her glass out for a refill.

He topped it off. "You don't know who your father is, do you?"

"Nope," she confessed. "Barely a clue."

It killed him that she wouldn't look at him. He didn't know if it stemmed from embarrassment or shame or the simple fact she was hanging on to her self-control by a thread. Maybe all of those reasons.

He took a stab in the dark. "I gather he's the one you're looking for."

She saluted him with her glass. "Right again."

"So what's his name? If you'd like, I'll pass it on to Juice and we'll have him tracked down in no time."

"Well, now, there's the hitch."

Rafe winced. "No name."

"No name," she confirmed.

"I can't think of a tactful way of asking my next question."

She jumped into the breach. "Then, let me ask it for you. Did my mother even know who he was? Yes, as a matter of fact, she did."

"And she won't give you his name?" Outrage rippled through Rafe's voice.

"She died before she got around to it, although she did let it slip one time that he lived in San Francisco. And Gran remembered her calling him Rory."

"Granted, that's not a lot to go on," Rafe conceded. "Even so, Juice may be able to help. Was there anything else? Letters, perhaps, or mementos?"

"You don't want to go there, Rafe," she whispered.

"Of course I want to go there. If it'll help—"

She set her glass on the raft with exquisite care. "Remember when I told you that my plan for an exit strategy from our engagement was on automatic? If you keep asking questions, the countdown begins."

"What the hell does finding your father have to do with ending our engagement?"

Darkness filled her eyes, turning them sooty with pain. "I can explain, if you insist. But don't forget I did try to warn you."

"Fine. You warned me. Now, what's going on?"

"My father gave my mother a bracelet shortly before she left him. I was going to use it to try to find him, assuming he wants to be found. It was unusual enough that it might help identify him."

"Go on."

"It was an antique bracelet."

"Great. So we'll give Juice the bracelet—"

She cut him off. "Small problem." He could see her struggle to maintain her composure. "I don't have it."

"Did you sell it?"

"*No!* Never."

"Then where is it?"

"My sister took it. My *half*-sister."

Son of a bitch. Did he have to drag every last detail out of her? "Okay, I really don't understand. How did she end up with your father's bracelet if he wasn't her father and the two of you didn't grow up together?"

"Every once in a while, Mom would drop by for a visit with my sister in tow. On one of the visits, Mom gave me the bracelet. My sister— *half*-sister—was not happy. She had everything money could buy, except that one thing. And she wanted it. It ate at her. I realize now she couldn't stand the idea that I possessed something she didn't. She threw a temper tantrum to end all temper tantrums."

"And your mother gave in? She gave the bracelet to your sister?"

"Nope. She dragged my sister, kicking and screaming, out of my grandmother's house. The few times they visited after that everything seemed fine, though one time I caught her snooping around in my room. But years later, long after Mom died, she showed up out of the blue. I thought it was an attempt to mend fences and reconnect." Larkin's laugh held more pain than amusement. "After she left, I discovered the bracelet had left with her."

"Can you get it back?"

"I don't know yet. Maybe."

"Is there anything I can do to help? Perhaps if we were to approach her, offer to purchase it?"

For some reason the kindness in his voice provoked a flood of tears and it took her a minute to control them. "Thanks."

"Aw, hell."

He swept her into his arms and she buried her face against his shoulder, her body curving into his. He couldn't understand how a parent could abandon her child. But then, he couldn't imagine making any of the choices Larkin's mother had. No wonder Larkin took such delight in his family and the way they encouraged and supported and—yes—interfered in each other's lives.

Larkin had never had any of that. Worse, she'd been abandoned by her mother, never known the love of her father, and been betrayed in the worst possible way by her sister. *Half-*sister. Well, that ended. Right now.

"We'll take care of this, sweetheart. We'll get your bracelet back and use it to track down your father. If anyone can do it, it's Juice." He pulled back slightly. "Let's start with finding the bracelet. What's your sister's name? Where does she live?"

Larkin caught him by surprise, ripping free of his embrace. Without a word she dived from the raft and struck out toward shore, cutting through the water as though all the demons of hell were close on her heels. He didn't hesitate. He gave chase, reaching the shore only steps behind her. Catching her by the shoulder, he spun her around.

"What the hell is going on?" he demanded, the air heaving in and out of his lungs. "Why did you take off like that?"

She struggled to catch her breath. Water ran in thin rivulets down her face, making it impossible to tell whether it was from her swim or from tears. "I warned you. I warned you not to go there."

A hideous suspicion took hold. "Who is she, Larkin? Who has your bracelet? *What's her name?*"

"Her name is . . . *was* . . . Leigh."

"Leigh," he repeated. He shook his head. "Not my late wife. Not *that* Leigh."

She closed her eyes and all the fight drained from her. "Yes, your late wife, Leigh. She was also my half-sister." She looked at him then, her eyes—those stunning aquamarine eyes—empty of all emotion. "And I wondered, assuming it's not too much trouble, if you could give me back the bracelet she took from me."

For a split second Rafe couldn't move, couldn't even think. Then comprehension stormed through him. "All this time you've been with me, you've kept your relationship to Leigh a secret? All so you could find her bracelet?"

"*My* bracelet. And no! Well, yes." She thrust her hands into her wet hair in open frustration, standing the curls on end. "I didn't move in with you in order to search for it, if that's what you're suggesting. But yes. I asked to be assigned to the Dantes reception in order to get an initial impression of you. To decide the best way to approach you."

She'd been sizing him up. Right from the start she'd been figuring out the perfect bait for her trap. And he'd fallen for it. Fallen for almost the exact same routine Leigh had used on him. The poor innocent waif. In Larkin's case, abandoned by her mother, searching for her father. Raised by her grandmother. Was any of it true? None of Leigh's stories had been. Or was this Larkin's clever way to get her hands on whatever valuables his late wife had left behind?

"What a fool I've been."

"I'm sorry, Rafe. To be honest—"

"Oh, by all means," he cut in sarcastically. "Do be honest. It would make such a refreshing change."

"I was going to tell you the truth the night you offered me a job."

He paced in front of her, more angry than he could ever remember being. Somehow Larkin had gotten under his skin in a way that Leigh never had, making the betrayal that much worse. "If you had told me that night, I'd have thrown you out then and there."

"I know."

"So you didn't mention it."

Her mouth tilted to one side in a wry smile. "I think it had more to do with your asking me to be your fiancée and then kissing me. That pretty much blew every other thought out of my head."

The fact his reaction had been identical to hers only served to increase his anger and frustration. "You still should have told me."

"Then your grandparents arrived on the scene and I got kicked out of my apartment." She continued the recital with relentless tenacity. "Maybe I should have confessed then, but to be hon—" She winced. "The reason I didn't was because I didn't feel like spending a night on the streets."

"I wouldn't have thrown you out in the middle of the night." He smiled grimly. "At least, I don't think so."

"Then in the morning I got swept off by Elia and Nonna. I really didn't want to make the announcement in front of them." She captured her lower lip between her teeth and a line of anxiety appeared between her brows. "But I shouldn't have let them spend any money on me. That was totally wrong, and if it's the last thing I do, I'll repay every dime."

"Would you forget about the damn money?" Rafe broke off and scrubbed his hands across his face. What the hell was he saying? Money was the reason she was here. She just had a different routine than Leigh, a far more effective one, as it turned out. "You had ample opportunity to tell me in the time we've been together. Why didn't you?"

She squared her shoulders. They looked breathtakingly delicate and feminine in her halter-top bathing suit—a fact he couldn't help but notice despite all that stood between them. "You're right. I should have told you. My only excuse is that I knew it would change everything between us." Her chin quivered before she brought it under ruthless control. "And I didn't want our relationship to change."

He did his best to ignore the chin. She might look like a helpless stray, but he didn't doubt she was every bit as conniving as her sister. Blood will tell, as Primo always said. Of course, he'd been referring to The Inferno. But maybe greed and deceit and a lack of honor ran in some families the way The Inferno ran in his. Like mother, like daughter.

"You want Leigh's bracelet? Fine. You'll have it first thing tomorrow. After that, I expect you to clear out."

His final comment kept her from replying for a moment. Her distress shouldn't affect him. Not anymore. But for some reason it did. "Then you have it?" she asked in a low voice. "I wasn't sure whether it had been lost when Leigh's plane went down."

"It was at Dantes at the time, having the catch repaired. Right now, it's in my office safe." He whistled for Kiko, then inclined his head toward the lake house. "Come on. We're leaving.

I'll tell everyone there's been an unexpected emergency."

She didn't argue. "Of course." Her tone turned formal. "I'll find somewhere else to stay as soon as we get back to the city."

The comment only served to spin his anger to an all-time high. "As much as I'd love to have you gone, it'll be far too late to find a place for both you and Kiko tonight. Tomorrow I'll get your damn bracelet and find you a hotel or apartment willing to house you both." He cut her off before she could argue. "Enough, Larkin. This discussion is over. From now on, we do things my way. And my way means you're out of my life as soon as I can arrange it."

Rafe didn't waste any time putting his plan into motion. Nor did he give his family the chance to do more than express confused concern before he had the two of them and Kiko packed and loaded and flying down the road toward San Francisco.

The instant they arrived home, Larkin made a beeline for her bedroom. Rafe followed. It wasn't the smartest move, but he had some final questions he wanted answered. He paused in the doorway, struggling to see through the pretense to the woman she'd revealed herself to be—a woman ruled by greed and avarice and dishonesty.

Day Leclaire

It was as though she read his mind. "I'm nothing like Leigh." She threw the comment over her shoulder.

"No? Time will tell." He stared at her, broodingly. "Once I slipped a ring on your sister's finger she went from sweet and innocent—like you—to cold and calculating. I have to hand it to her, she put on a great act leading up to our wedding. I guess I'm an easy mark when it comes to the helpless waif type of woman. Leigh was a more sophisticated version, granted, but that changed soon enough. It didn't take long to realize she wanted what every other woman wants from a Dante, the good life and everything my money could provide. I suppose I could have lived with that. For a while."

"Then what went wrong?"

"It was the adultery that I refused to tolerate."

The fluid lines of Larkin's body stiffened and she slowly turned to face him. "She cheated on you? *You?*"

He supposed he should be flattered by the way she said that. "Hard to imagine?"

"Yes, it is."

His eyes narrowed and he approached, swallowing up the narrow bones of her shoulders in his two hands. "How do you do it?"

She stared up at him, eyes huge and startling blue, her expression one of stark innocence. Bambi in human form. "Do what?"

"Look the way you do, so trustworthy and ingenuous, when everything you say is a total lie. How do you do that?"

"I'm not Leigh." She spoke calmly enough, but a hint of steel and temper washed across her face. "You're trying to tuck us into the same little box and I refuse to allow it. *I am not Leigh!*"

"And I might have believed you if you'd been candid about your connection to Leigh from the start. Just out of curiosity, was any of your story true? Were you really abandoned by your mother and raised by your grandmother?"

Exhaustion lined her face, along with a heart-wrenching despair. "I've never lied to you, Rafe. I simply didn't tell you about Leigh and the bracelet. I even told you I had secrets. Omissions. Remember?" She searched his face, probably looking for some weakness she could use to her advantage. "You said lying by omission was part of dating. Everything else I told you was the truth."

"And I'm supposed to just believe it."

"You know what, Rafe? I don't care what you believe. I know it's the truth and that's all that matters." She lifted her chin an inch. "You should be grateful to me, you know that? I've given you the perfect excuse for staying emotionally disconnected. I betrayed you. Now you can go back to being independent. The original lone wolf. You should be celebrating."

"Somehow I don't feel like celebrating." She attempted to pull back and he tightened his hold, his voice dropping to a whisper. "I can still feel it. Why is that?"

She didn't pretend to misunderstand. A hint of panic crept into her gaze, combining with a wealth of longing. "Maybe it really is The Inferno."

"You'd love that, wouldn't you?"

She hesitated. "I'd love it if it were real," she admitted with brutal frankness. "But I'm not that thrilled about it given the current circumstances."

He uttered a humorless laugh. "There's one good thing that's come from all this."

Her breath escaped her lungs in a soft rush. "I'm afraid to ask . . . ."

"Once I explain the facts to my family, they'll finally leave me alone. No more Inferno possibilities paraded beneath my nose. Not only that, but they'll understand completely why I can't marry my Inferno soul mate. How could I, when she's Leigh's sister?"

Bone-deep temper ignited in Larkin's eyes, turning the color to an incandescent shade of cobalt-blue. *"Half*-sister. And I'm getting really, *really* tired of being hanged for her crimes. You want something to be angry about? I'll give you something."

She swept her hands up across his chest and into his hair. Grabbing two thick handfuls, she yanked his face down to hers and took his mouth in a ruthless kiss. Desire roared through him at her aggressiveness. Her mouth slanted across his, hot and damp with passion. Gently she parted his lips with hers. Teasing. Offering. Beckoning him inward. He didn't hesitate.

He tugged her closer, melding them together. Her thighs, strong and slender, slipped between his while her pelvis curved snugly against him. He could feel the shape and softness of her breasts against his chest, feel the pebbled tips that spoke of her need. And her mouth. Her mouth tasted as sweet and lush and delicious as a ripe peach.

He staggered forward a step, falling with her onto the bed. The instant they hit the mattress, he shoved his hands up under her shirt and cupped the pert apple roundness of her breasts. He traced his thumbs across her rigid nipples, catching her hungry moan in his mouth. The sound was the final straw.

He lost himself. Lost himself in the fire that erupted every time they touched. She wrapped her legs around him, pulling him tighter against her. Her breath came in frantic little gasps and she snatched quick bites of his mouth.

"Tell me this is a lie," she demanded. "Tell me I'm lying about what happens whenever you kiss me. Tell me this isn't real."

It took endless seconds for her words to penetrate. The instant they did, he swore viciously. "Not again."

"Yes, again." She wiggled out from underneath him and shot to her feet. "Do you think I want it to happen? You're Leigh's husband. I've never before wanted anything that belonged to her. But you—" Her voice broke and she turned away.

"I never belonged to her."

"You were married to her." She lifted a shoulder in a disconsolate shrug. "There's not much difference as far as I can tell."

He stood, aware nothing he could do or say would restore order to his world. He wanted a woman he didn't trust, probably would have made love to her again if she hadn't put a stop to it before it went any further. He'd already had his life turned upside down once, courtesy of his former wife. He wasn't about to let it happen again.

"I don't belong to any woman. And I never will."

"A lone wolf to the end?" she whispered.

"It's better than the alternative."

With that he turned and left. And all the while his palm burned, screaming in protest.

Chapter Ten

Larkin spent the night curled up in the middle of the bed counting the minutes until dawn.

Rafe was right about one thing. She should have told him she was Leigh's sister—*half-sister*—right from the start. That had been the plan all along. If only she hadn't gotten distracted. No, time to face the truth. She hadn't been all that distracted. She hadn't wanted to reveal her identity to him because living the lie had filled her with more joy than she'd ever before experienced.

She swiped at her cheeks, despising the fact that they were damp with tears. She'd discovered at an early age that feeling sorry for herself didn't help. Nor did it change anything. Not that she had much to feel sorry about. She'd had Gran, who'd been a wonderful substitute parent.

Even so, she'd be kidding herself if she didn't acknowledge that some small part of her felt as though she were always on the outside looking in. That she'd never quite measured up. More than anything, she'd wanted to be loved by her mother. To belong. To have known the love of a father, as well. Instead, what had Leigh called her? A Mistake. Capital A. Capital M. Underlined and italicized. As a result, Larkin had held men at a distance, determined not to visit upon a new generation the same mistakes of her parents. If you didn't fall in love, you couldn't create A Mistake.

But her lack of a real family, a "normal" family, one that consisted of more than a loving grandmother, had filled her with an intense restlessness, a need to belong. Somewhere. To someone. To find the elusive dream of hearth and home and family. To finally fit in. But how did you find that when you were too wary to let people approach? Beside her, Kiko whimpered and bellied in closer.

"I know I wasn't a mistake, any more than you were," she told the dog. "We just don't quite fit in anywhere. We're unique. Special. Caught between two worlds, neither of our own making."

But no matter how hard her grandmother had tried to convince her of that fact and fill her life with love, there'd always been a part of her that had conceded there was a certain element of truth to Leigh's words. Bottom line, she wasn't good enough for her mother to keep. She'd been thrown away. Dispensable.

Until Rafe.

For a brief shining time she'd discovered what it meant to belong to a family, one who'd welcomed her with open arms. Until she'd ruined it. "I should have told him." Kiko whined in what Larkin took as agreement. "But then he'd never have made love to me. And I'd never have fallen in love with him."

Tears escaped no matter how hard she tried to prevent them. It was worth it, she kept repeating to herself. No matter how badly it ended, the days she'd had with Rafe were worth the agony to come. If she had to do it all over again, she would.

Without a minute's hesitation.

Dawn finally arrived, giving Rafe the excuse he needed to give up on pretending to sleep and dress for work. He would have skipped breakfast, but Kiko padded out to join him, and well, damn it. He couldn't let the poor girl starve, could he?

He didn't see or hear any sign of Larkin, which was fine by him. The sooner he concluded their remaining business, the sooner he could get his life onto an even keel again. Go back to the way things had been before Larkin had stormed into his life and ripped it to shreds. Avoid further emotional entanglements and just be left the hell alone.

"It's what I've always wanted," he informed Kiko.

She gave his comment the attention it deserved, which was none at all. Aware he didn't have a hope in hell of gaining any support from that quarter, he downed the last of his coffee and rinsed the mug. Then, refusing to consider the whys and wherefores of his actions, he started up a fresh pot before heading out the door.

He wasn't expected at the office, since the entire Dante family was still officially on vacation. He'd also given his assistant the time off, which provided him complete privacy to closet himself in his office, undisturbed. He wasted a couple of hours taking care of business emails and paperwork, knowing full well they were his way of avoiding the inevitable. Finally, he shoved back his chair and stared at the display rack that concealed his office safe.

He sighed. Just get it over with!

It took him only minutes to punch in the appropriate code and verify his thumbprint. The door swung open and he sorted through the various gemstones and jewelry samples stored there until he found the plain rectangular box he'd stashed in the farthest recesses.

Removing it, he relocked the safe and carried the box to his desk. Flipping open the lid, he stared down at the bracelet. It was a stunning piece. The setting gave the impression of spun gold, delicate filigree links that appeared to be straight out of a fairy tale. The original stones had been a lovely mixture of modest diamonds of a decent quality, and amethysts that weren't bad, if a shade on the pink side. Not good enough for Leigh, of course, but then few things were.

She'd insisted he replace the amethysts with emeralds because they were her birthstone, and the smaller diamonds with oversize fire diamonds because they were more impressive, not to mention expensive. He'd never felt either complemented the setting. But since he'd still been in the throes of lust, he'd agreed to her demands. She'd even wanted to have the setting altered, but there he'd drawn the line. It was perfect as is. Instead, she'd gone behind his back and made the adjustments without his knowledge. It wouldn't take much to return it to its original form, he decided, studying the bracelet. Sev's wife, Francesca, could do it in her sleep.

A knock sounded at the door and his sister, Gia, poked her head into his office. "Hey, you. Larkin said I could find you here."

He leaned back in his chair. "Did she, now."

"Yes, she did."

Gia entered the room and closed the door behind her. He and his sister had always been dubbed the "pretty" Dantes, identical in coloring, with matching jade-green eyes. While he'd despised the moniker, Gia had simply shrugged it off, neither impressed nor dismayed by the description. He, on the other hand, had been offended on her behalf, since his sister wasn't merely pretty. She was flat-out gorgeous.

"To be honest, I'm relieved Larkin's still at your place," she continued. "When the two of you left the lake, I was a little worried you were on the verge of breaking up."

"So you followed us home?" Her shrug spoke volumes. "It's none of your business, Gianna."

"Then you *are* on the verge of breaking up. Oh, Rafe." She approached and slid a slim hip onto the edge of his desk. Leaning in, she examined the bracelet. A delaying tactic, no doubt. "Huh. Definitely not Francesca's work. Almost beautiful. Or it would be if it weren't so—" she made a fluttering gesture with her hands "—over the top. It also needs softer stones."

"Amethysts."

"Exactly." She nodded, impressed. "Good eye. Whose is it?"

"Leigh's." He corrected himself. "Larkin's, I guess."

Confusion lined Gia's brow. "Come again?"

"Leigh and Larkin are sisters. *Half*-sisters." Though why he bothered to make the distinction he couldn't say.

Gia's mouth dropped open. "Is this some sort of joke?"

"I wish." He gave her the short version. "Now she wants her bracelet. Once she has it, she'll be on her way. She can use it to try to find her father, or sell it, or do whatever the hell she wants with it." He flipped the case closed with a loud snap. "And that brings to an end my very brief Inferno engagement."

"I don't understand. Why does any of that put an end to your engagement?"

He glared at his sister. "What do you mean, why? Because she's Leigh's sister." He grimaced. *"Half*-sister."

"So? It's not like she's Leigh. You only have to talk to her for five minutes to realize that much."

"She lied to me."

"Did she? She claimed she wasn't Leigh's sister?"

"Half-sister," he muttered.

"I'll take that as a no." She waited for him to say more, blowing out her breath in exasperation when he remained stubbornly silent. "Fine. Be that way. But you can tell Larkin that if she needs somewhere to stay while she searches for her father—"

"Assuming there is a father and she's actually searching for him."

Gia inclined her head. "Assuming all that. She's welcome to crash at my place." She slipped off the desk. "Larkin loves you, you know."

He stilled. "She used me."

Gia shrugged. "It happens. But I'll tell you one thing . . ." She paused on her way out the door. For some reason she wouldn't look at him. "I'd give anything to have what you're throwing away."

Rafe returned home to find Larkin perched on the edge of a chair in his living room, dressed in one of her old outfits. Kiko lay at her feet, the dog's graying muzzle resting on her paws. Her brilliant gold eyes shifted in Rafe's direction and she watched him with unnerving intensity. He caught a similar expression in Larkin's gaze. Beside the dog sat her backpack. It didn't take much thought to add two and two and come up with . . . Larkin was running. At least she'd done him the courtesy of waiting until he returned home. But then, it wasn't likely she'd leave without her bracelet.

She drew in a deep breath and blew it out. Rising, she gathered up her backpack, shifting it nervously from hand to hand. "Do you have it?"

He removed the box from his suit-jacket pocket and held it out to her. Without a word she accepted it and turned her back on him, her spine rigid and unrelenting.

"That's it?" he asked, though he didn't know what more he expected.

"Thanks." She threw the words over her shoulder. "But if it's all the same with you, Kiko and I will be on our way now."

He let her go. It was better this way. Easier. Cleaner. Safer.

An instant later she slammed her backpack to the ground. Whirling around, she came charging toward him. "Rafaelo Dante, what the hell have you done to my bracelet?" She shook the box he'd given her under his nose. "What are you trying to pull? You were supposed to give me *my* bracelet. Not this . . . this . . . *thing.*"

"That is your bracelet."

Larkin popped open the top and held out the glittering spill of gold and gems. "Look at it, Rafe. What happened to it? It's ruined!"

How was it possible that she could put him on the defensive with such ease? "Leigh had me switch out the stones. Don't worry. It's even more valuable than it was before."

"Valuable? *Valuable!*" She stared at him as though he'd grown two heads. "What has that got to do with anything?"

"I just thought—"

Larkin's eyes hardened, filling with a cynicism he'd never seen there before. And something else. Something that twisted him into knots and filled him with shame. It was disillusionment he read in her gaze. It was as though he'd told her there was no Santa Claus. No Easter Bunny. No magic or fairies or wishing on stars. As though he'd taken every last hope and dream and crushed it beneath his heel.

"I know what you thought," she stated in a raw, husky voice. "You assumed I'm like Leigh. That it's the dollar-and-cent worth of an item that's important."

It hit him then. She wasn't Leigh. How could he ever have thought she was? It was like comparing an angel to a viper. Where Leigh had demanded and taken, Larkin had given him the most precious possession she owned—herself. And he'd thrown that gift back in her face. Accused her of the worst possible crime—being the same as her sister. *Half*-sister. She'd given him her heart and he'd tossed it aside as though it were worthless, just as her mother had done.

"Don't you get it?" she whispered. Pain carved deep lines in her expression. "This bracelet is my only connection to my father. How am I supposed to use it to find him when it looks nothing like he remembers?"

Rafe flinched. *Face it, Dante, you screwed up.* And now he had a choice, a choice that was vanishing with each passing moment. One path led back the way he'd come. Returned him to where he'd been just weeks ago. The other option . . .

Well, if he chose that one, he'd have to risk everything he'd always considered most precious. His independence. His need to control his world and everything within it. The barriers he'd spent a lifetime erecting to protect himself.

But the potential reward . . .

He looked at Larkin. Truly looked at her. That's all it took. He burrowed the thumb of his left hand into the throbbing center of his right palm and surrendered to the inevitable. He'd risk it all. Risk anything to have her back in his life. And just like that, a plan fell into place. It would take days to accomplish, possibly weeks. It would take extreme delicacy and exquisite timing. But it just might work.

Now for step one. "I can put the bracelet back the way it was," he offered.

Tears welled up and she brushed at them with a short, angry motion. "Forget it. I don't want anything from you."

She turned to leave, whistling to Kiko. Instead of following, the dog darted forward, snatched the backpack in her jaws and took off at a dead run up the steps to the second story.

"Kiko!" she and Rafe called in unison.

Together they raced after her, finding her crouched in the center of his bed, guarding the backpack. She barked at the pair of them.

"Looks like she doesn't want you to leave," Rafe said.

"She'll get over it." Larkin approached the bed and picked up the backpack. "Let's go, Kiko."

Though the dog allowed Larkin to take the backpack, she hunkered down on the bed in a position that clearly stated she wasn't planning to budge anytime soon. Okay, this could work to his advantage.

"Let her stay," Rafe suggested.

"What?" Larkin turned on him. "Why?"

"You both can stay here until we get the problem of your bracelet sorted out."

She instantly shook her head. "That's not going to happen."

Rafe wasn't surprised. That would have been too easy, and something told him nothing about regaining her trust would prove easy. "In that case, Gia has offered you a room while you search for your father. The only problem is that her place isn't suitable for Kiko. Leave her here for the time being."

Tears filled Larkin's eyes. "It's not enough you ruined my bracelet? Now you're taking my dog, too?"

Hell. "I'm not taking her," he explained patiently. "I'm letting her stay until our business is settled."

Her chin jutted out. "I thought our business was settled."

"Apparently not. I still owe you for your time and the damage to the bracelet."

"Forget it."

"Somehow I had a feeling you were going to say that," he muttered. "In that case, the least I can do is have your bracelet fixed so it's returned to its original condition. Will you consider that a fair exchange?"

She looked doubtful. "You can do that?"

"Francesca can handle anything."

"Francesca." Her eyes widened at the reminder, filling with horror. "I forgot about the engagement ring."

She yanked the ring off, holding it out to him. When he refused to take it, she crossed to his bedside table and placed it there with unmistakable finality. "If you'll have my bracelet repaired, I'll consider us even."

He wouldn't. Not by a long shot. She squared her shoulders and turned her back on Kiko. The expression on her face almost brought him to his knees. Despite the love and support she'd received from her grandmother, everyone else in her life had abandoned her. So many rejections in such a short life. And here it was happening to her again.

Well, not for long. No matter what it took, he intended to make things right.

The next couple of weeks were absolute agony for Larkin. Rafe made no attempt to get in touch. Nor did she go to the house, even though she missed Kiko fiercely. She made noises a couple of times about sneaking over while Rafe was at work so she could see her dog, but Gia claimed her brother had elected to stay at home for the remainder of his vacation, and Larkin couldn't bring herself to confront him. At least, not yet. Not while recent events were still so raw.

Midway through the third week, word finally came that the repairs to her bracelet were completed. "Meet me downstairs in five and I'll drive you over," Gia called to say. "I think I'm almost as excited as you to see how it looks."

It wasn't until they made the turn onto Rafe's street that Larkin realized where they were going. "I thought the bracelet would be at Dantes," she said uneasily.

"Nope. Rafe has it." Gia spared her an impatient look. "You've done nothing but grouse about the fact that you haven't seen Kiko in weeks. Now you have the opportunity to see both her and the bracelet. You should be over the moon. Don't tell me you're going to let a little thing like my good-for-nothing brother spoil your big moment."

"No. No, of course I won't." Maybe not.

To her surprise, Gia pulled up in front. Instead of parking, she waved her hand toward the house. "On second thought, why don't you go ahead without me."

Larkin turned to glare. "You're setting me up, aren't you? You think if I go in there alone, maybe Rafe and I will resolve our differences."

Gia shrugged. "Worth a try."

"It's not going to work."

"Then it won't work. But at least I'll have given it a shot."

Realizing it was pointless to argue, Larkin exited the car. Snatching a deep breath, she forced herself to climb the steps of the front porch at a sedate pace and knock. A minute later the door swung open and Rafe stood there. They stared at each other for an endless moment before he stepped back to allow her to pass.

She didn't know what to say. Emotions flooded through her. Powerful emotions. Longing. Regret mixed with sorrow. Love and the sheer futility of that love. And overriding them all was pain. A bone-deep, all-invasive hurt.

"Where's Kiko?" she managed to ask.

"Out back." For some reason he couldn't seem to take his eyes off her, his gaze practically eating her alive. "The gentleman who brought the bracelet wanted you to inspect it before he left and I wasn't sure how well he'd take to having a wolf hovering over him."

She almost smiled, catching herself at the last instant. "But Kiko's okay?"

"She's fine. Misses you. But then, that seems to be going around."

She blinked up at him, not quite sure what to make of his comment. Not that his expression gave anything away. "I guess we shouldn't keep your associate waiting."

Rafe led the way to the den and shoved open the door. She could see her bracelet spread out across the empty glass-topped desk, captured within the beam of a bright spotlight. A man stood nearby, silent and attentive.

Larkin approached the table, her breath catching when she saw the bracelet. She swung around to glance at Rafe, tears gathering in her eyes. "It's beautiful. Please tell Francesca she did an amazing job restoring it."

The man beside the table cleared his throat. "She made a few minor changes. The fire diamonds, for instance. They're similar in size, but the quality can't be compared. And I understand she used Verdonia Royal amethysts. The color is stunning, don't you think?"

Larkin glanced at the man and smiled. "Don't tell Francesca, but I still prefer the original."

"Do you really?"

For some reason, he seemed ridiculously pleased by the comment. He looked directly at her then and she froze, riveted. He was far shorter than Rafe, maybe five foot six or seven and somewhere in his late forties. Eyes the color of aquamarines twinkled behind a pair of wire-rimmed glasses. And though his wheat-white hair was cut short, there was no disguising the wayward curls that were next to impossible to subdue. His nose was different from hers, stubbier, but they shared the same pointed chin and wide mouth. And she knew without even spending a minute of time with him that he used that mouth to laugh. A lot. Best of all, he made her think of leprechauns and rainbows and pots of gold. And he made her think of magic and the possibility of dreams coming true.

"I must confess," he said, "the old girl looks quite grand with all those fancy stones attached to her."

Larkin continued to stare at him, unable to look away. "Old girl?" she repeated faintly.

"The bracelet. She belonged to your great-great-great-grandmother."

"You're—"

"Rory Finnegan. I'm your father, Larkin."

She never remembered moving. One minute she was standing next to the table and the next she was in his arms. "Dad?"

"You have no idea how long I've been looking for you." He whispered the words into her ear and they flowed straight to her heart.

The next few hours flashed by. At some point, Larkin realized Rafe had slipped away, giving her and her father some much-needed privacy. Coffee would periodically appear at their elbow, along with sandwiches. But she never noticed who brought them, though it didn't take much guesswork to know Rafe was behind that, too.

During the time she spent with her father, she discovered her mother had called him shortly before her death. "She was horribly sick. Almost incoherent," he explained. "She just kept telling me I had a daughter but couldn't give me a name or location. By the time I tracked her down, she was gone and that bastard of a husband claimed he had no idea what I was talking about."

Larkin also learned her name belonged to the same woman whose bracelet she'd been given. And she discovered she had a family as extensive as the Dantes, and every bit as lovingly nosy. "You won't be able to get rid of us," Rory warned. "Not now that I've found you. I'd have brought a whole herd of the troublemakers with me, but I didn't want to overwhelm you."

When the time finally came for him to leave, they were both teary eyed. Standing by the front door, he snatched her close for a tight hug. "You'll come by this weekend. We'll throw a big welcome home party. And bring your man with you. Your grandmother Finnegan will want to give him the once over before okaying the wedding date."

"Oh, but—"

"We'll be there," Rafe informed him, joining them.

The instant the door closed behind her father, Larkin turned to confront Rafe. "I don't know what to say," she confessed, fighting back tears. "Thank you seems so inadequate."

"You're welcome." He held out his hand. "I have something else I want to show you."

"Okay." She dared to slip her hand into his, closing her eyes when The Inferno throbbed in joyous welcome. "But then I'd really like to see Kiko."

"That's what I wanted to show you."

He pulled her toward the back of the house to the guest suite where she'd spent so many blissful days and nights. The door was shut and on the wooden surface someone had screwed a glistening gold placard. "Official Den of Tukiko and Youko" it read.

"You told me that was Kiko's full name. I looked up the meaning." He slanted her a flashing smile. "Moon child?"

Larkin shrugged. "It seemed fitting." She frowned at the sign. "But who is Youko?"

"Ah, you mean our sun child."

He shoved open the door. Where once had stood a regular bed, now there were two huge dog beds. The door to the backyard stood ajar and he ushered her in that direction. She gaped at the changes. In the time she'd been gone, someone had come through and transformed the yard into a giant doggy playpen. Rope pulls and exercise rings, doghouses and toys were scattered throughout the area. He'd even had a section of lawn dug up and a giant square of loosely packed dirt put in its place.

"For digging," he explained. "And burying bones. And for rolling around, if that's what they want."

Just then Kiko emerged from one of the doghouses and bounded across to her side, nearly bowling them both down in her enthusiasm. Larkin wrapped her arms around her dog and buried her face in the thick ruff.

"I've missed you so much." A small whine drew her attention back to the doghouse. Peeking out from the shadows was another animal. "And who is this?" Kiko darted back to stand protectively beside the newcomer, a dog who appeared to be part yellow Lab and part golden retriever. "Youko, I presume?"

"She's a rescue dog. Terrified of people, so I'm assuming she was abused. Kiko's helping me socialize her." He hesitated. "I'm hoping you'll help, too."

She stiffened. "A dog's a big responsibility. A long-term commitment."

"Fifteen, twenty years, if we're lucky. Of course, Kiko's Pals will also be a long-term commitment."

Larkin stared blankly. "Kiko's Pals?"

"It's the rescue organization we're starting, if you're willing. A charitable organization to help dogs like Kiko. I'm hoping you'll run it."

"You've started—" She broke off, fighting for control. "You did that for her? For us?"

"I'd do anything for the two of you," he stated simply.

"I don't understand," she whispered. "I don't understand any of this."

"Then let me explain."

This time he took her upstairs, pausing outside his bedroom door. Another plaque had been attached. This one read, "Den of the Big Bad Wolf and his Once in a Lifetime Mate." He opened the door and stepped back, giving her the choice of entering or walking away.

She didn't hesitate. She stepped across the threshold and straight into hope. He closed the door and she turned. In two swift steps he reached her side and pulled her into his arms.

"I'm so sorry, Larkin. I was an idiot. You're nothing like Leigh and never could be. I've spent so many years protecting myself that I almost lost the only thing I've ever wanted. You." He cupped her face and kissed her, losing himself in the scent and taste and feel of her. "I love you. I think I loved you from the first minute we touched."

"Oh, Rafe." She was laughing and crying at the same time. "I love you, too."

He pulled back. "I still want you to be my temporary fiancée."

Her eyes narrowed. "You do, huh?"

"Definitely. A very temporary fiancée, followed by a very long-term wife." He swung her into his arms and carried her to the bed. "You'll have to remind me where we left off. It's been so long I can't quite remember."

She wrapped her arms around his neck and feathered a kiss across his mouth. "I'll see what I can do to refresh your memory."

"Nope. We can't do that. Not without breaking my promise to Primo."

He fumbled for something on the dressing table. Taking her hand in his, he slid her engagement ring on her finger, back where it belonged. The heat of The Inferno flared between them and even though he didn't acknowledge it aloud, she could see the acceptance in his eyes.

"It would seem this is the perfect ring after all," he told her.

"And why is that?" she asked, even though she already knew.

"Your ring is named Once in a Lifetime, which is fitting because if there's one thing you've taught me—" he kissed her long and hard "—it's that wolves mate for life."

The Dante Inferno continues with Draco's story!

Draco's Marriage Pact by Day Leclaire

Meet Day Leclaire

I love family first and foremost, which is why writing a family saga is so much fun. Maybe you can tell that from my books since they always feature the warmth and joy that comes from having a close-knit family. I also love animals and have taken in rescue dogs and cats and fostered dogs for the local animal shelter. And of course, I love writing. All I need is a functioning brain (batteries not included), a pen, and paper, and I can write anywhere. Please don't let a conversation with me lag because my imagination takes over and I. Am. Checked. Out!

USA Today bestselling author, Day Leclaire is the author of more than 60 novels and has received an impressive eleven nominations for the romance industry's most prestigious award, Romance Writers of America RITA© Award. Day lives in Charlotte, NC and spends her days obsessively writing while vaguely remembering to pay attention to her adorable husband, busy son and daughter-in-law, two tiny grandchildren, and two even tinier Teddy Bear dogs. Not to mention a whole lot of dust!

Thank you so much for taking the time to read **The Dante Inferno:** *The Dante Dynasty Series*. I hope you enjoy this very special Italian-American family. I love hearing from my readers. For a personal response, please contact me at Day@DayLeclaire.com. And be sure to visit my website at www.DayLeclaire.com. Sign up for my newsletter for my latest releases and insider info available nowhere else! Just visit: https://www.dayleclaire.com/join-my-mailing-list

You can also find me on Facebook at www.facebook.com/Day.Leclaire.Private and Twitter at www.Twitter.com/DayLeclaire.